PEGGY GADDIS

The Girl Next Door

John Curley & Associates, Inc.
South Yarmouth, Ma.

Library of Congress Cataloging in Publication Data

Gaddis, Peggy
  The girl next door.

  1. Large type books. I. Title.
[PS3513.A227G5 1987]   813′.52   86–24300
ISBN 1–55504–199–X (lg. print)
ISBN 1–55504–266–X (pbk.: lg. print)

Published in Large Print by arrangement with Donald MacCampbell, Inc in the United States and territories; Canada and the rest of the world market.

Distributed in the U.K. and Commonwealth by Magna Print Books.

Printed in Great Britain

Chapter One

Betsy Drummond sat in the darkest corner of the old carriage house. Outside, a spring morning spread a mantle of beauty over the countryside. Meadows were green and soft with new grass; along the river, yellow-green willows bent over their graceful reflections.

And yet – in the old carriage house, Betsy Drummond shrank back, a black bandage over her eyes.

"This is what it's like to be blind," she told herself. "This is what Pete knows. Never to see again! Oh, Pete, darling, I can't stand it! Not for you, Pete."

Peter had loved beauty; he had loved to walk through the woods and fields in the spring. He had seen beauty even in bare fields, and had pointed out to Betsy the myriad color tones of the newly turned earth. And now – Peter was blind, hopelessly blind!

Betsy had fought against the knowledge since the morning, such a short while ago, that Peter's mother had stood before her, gray-faced and white-lipped, and told her the truth.

1

"We've got to help him, Betsy," Mrs. Marshall had said. "He doesn't want us to come to the hospital. He wants to come home alone. All we can do is wait till he's ready to come back to us."

Betsy shivered. She couldn't tell Mrs. Marshall that Peter would not be coming home to her – Betsy. Peter wasn't in love with her, never had been. They'd been pals, and had wrangled amicably. Betsy had tagged his footsteps until sometimes he had chased her home, as he would an annoying puppy.

Ever since she could remember, Betsy had loved Peter Marshall. But he had just grinned at her, called her "Carrot-top," pulled her pigtails, and teased her. Six years makes a terrific difference in ages when you're growing up. But Peter was twenty-four now, and Betsy was almost nineteen.

She had written to him faithfully through the long three years he'd been in Vietnam. She had written him daily, but she only mailed one letter a week. The others were put away in a small locked jewel box in the bottom of her bureau, where no one would ever see them. In these letters, she had poured out her young heart, revealing all its small inner secrets. In the letter she had let herself mail each week, she had been the

2

happy-go-lucky youngster he remembered. From the brief, scrawled answers he had sent her, she knew he still thought of her as the leggy, carrot-topped youngster she'd been when he went away.

Peter would never see her now, as she had grown up. Her hair was a rich mahogany-red, the coltish young figure had filled out; the golden-brown eyes were steady and honest, and the small line of freckles that marched across her impertinent little nose were almost hidden by the warm sun-tan that gave her such a healthy, wholesome look.

And soon now he was coming home – blind! She bowed her bandaged head on her knees and wept. . . .

She was so absorbed in her misery that she did not hear the protesting squeak with which the doors of the carriage house swung open. The warm flood of April sunlight could not penetrate the thick bandage over her eyes. It was not until a voice spoke that she started up so swiftly that her head struck a low beam. Her hands shook as she tore off the bandage.

A woman stood in the doorway, outlined by the sunlight. For a moment, Betsy's eyes were so blinded that she saw the figure only as a blur.

"Oh – hello," said the woman, obviously

startled. "Did I frighten you? I'm sorry. I had no idea anyone was here. The place looks as if nobody has been here in a hundred years or so."

"I – that is – it's the old Cunningham place," Betsy stammered. "It's been closed for years. I live next door."

Now that her eyes were focused against sunlight, she could see that the woman was attractive. Thick, shining dark hair was tucked into a roll that framed her face. She had large brown eyes, a warm-lipped mouth, and a straight, beautiful nose that made Betsy all the more conscious of the impertinent tilt of her own.

The woman, who was bareheaded, was wearing a smart suit of summer tweed, its jacket flung across her shoulders. The bright yellow sweater, which she wore in lieu of a blouse, seemed to accentuate her dark beauty.

"I'm Marcia Eldon," she said, and there was still a look of curiosity in her eyes as she took in the small, dejected figure in crumpled blue flannel shorts and white shirt. "I've rented the place for a year. I'm going to live here – that is, I suppose it will really be existing, not living." Her lips curled in a grimace of distaste.

Betsy's eyes widened. "You're going
4

to live here – in Centerville?" She repeated.

Marcia Eldon nodded; then her eyes swept the carriage house disparagingly. "I admit I haven't the faintest idea what you are doing here," she said, "but please feel free to use the place. I'm sure there's plenty of room for my car – and you, as well." She waited for Betsy to explain.

Betsy hesitated, and her face flushed. "Oh," she muttered unhappily, "I just came in here to – to think something out."

Marcia laughed and looked about the place, which was thick with dust, hung with cobwebs, and unmistakably a happy-hunting-ground for rats.

"It must have been something that required a lot of concentration," she drawled. "Or aren't you afraid of spiders and mice?"

"Of course not." Betsy turned toward the loose plank at the back, through which she always slipped. "I'll be seeing you around, I suppose," she said hurriedly, and pushed back the plank.

"You ridiculous child! Why not go out through the door?" exclaimed Marcia, annoyed.

But Betsy had already slipped through the opening, and was flying across what had once

5

been a vegetable garden, toward the tall hedge.

In her room, Betsy got out of the dusty shorts and the shirt, and her scuffed saddle shoes. She took a shower and dressed in a crisp cotton frock, tied her curls back with a ribbon, and ran down the front steps and out into the street. She was thankful to have escaped her mother, because she felt that she couldn't bear to talk to her. Mother was so gentle and understanding, but – to Betsy – even the kindest word was like a finger pressing upon an unbearable painful spot.

She chose back lanes and side streets as she hurried across town. Presently she came to a quiet little street that ended on a bluff above the river. Here a small, sturdy cottage sat in a thick grove of pines. Behind it were neat chicken runs, a few fruit trees and a small vegetable garden.

Betsy went up the walk and around the house to where rustic chairs were grouped beneath a giant water oak. Beyond it, a small garden flaunted all the heavily fragrant flowers one could imagine – gardenias, roses, spice-pinks....

An old man sat in one of the rustic chairs. His white head lifted alertly as Betsy came across the lawn, walking as quietly as she could. Before she reached him, he laughed and said:

"Betsy, my dear, how nice to see you!"

Betsy smiled uncertainly.

"I never get over being surprised that you know who it is, before I so much as open my mouth," she told him, dropping down in a chair beside him.

The old man's sightless eyes were turned toward her and his smile was friendly and fond.

"That's because when one loses the sense of sight, my dear, the other senses are intensified. There are no two people on earth whose footsteps are exactly alike; just as no two voices are identical. You've been crying, Betsy," he added quietly.

There was a hint of reproach in his voice and Betsy's face crumpled, although she tried hard not to weep.

"I'm sorry, Professor. I – I've *tried* – like the dickens."

He nodded. "I know you have, my dear. It's very hard. But when Peter comes, you want to be brave and strong, to help him. If he sees you crying – "

"I won't let him see me – " She broke off and set her teeth tight in her lower lip. It wouldn't be hard to keep Peter from seeing, she reflected, unhappily. He would never see again!

Professor Hartley said, "Don't you want to see Tamar's son? He's developing beautifully."

"Oh, yes!" Betsy agreed, and some of her pain and misery vanished.

The old man whistled and two dogs came leaping towards him. One was a full-grown German shepherd; the other, a half-grown pup. The grown dog paused at the professor's knee and his hand reached out and caressed her. The puppy frolicked a moment, but at a word from the man, he came obediently and the thin old hands fitted a harness to his shoulders.

"Try him out, Betsy," suggested the professor.

She bound a handkerchief over her eyes, put her hand on the curved wooden harness above the dog's shoulders and he walked her patiently about the garden, skilfully avoiding trees, bushes, any obstacle in their path. Even when she exerted pressure on the harness, the dog could not be forced to walk into any obstruction.

She whipped off the handkerchief, knelt and put her arms about the young dog, fondling him. There were tears in her eyes and in her voice as she talked to him.

8

"He's a darling, Professor," she said. "You've been swell to give him to me and to help me train him for Pete."

"I can only hope he will give Peter the comfort and companionship his mother has given me. Come here, Betsy."

She released the dog, took off the harness, and went to sit beside the old man.

"You're growing up, Betsy," he said gently. "Sorrow makes one adult far more than years. You're facing up, and I'm proud of you."

Betsy set her teeth hard. "I'm not the one that needs to be brave," she said unsteadily. "It's Pete – "

"And don't you think he will be?"

"Oh – of course."

"Betsy, you must realize one thing." The professor's voice was quiet, but there was a ring of conviction in it. "There are compensations, even for blindness. Perhaps you never see beauty again – but you can never forget it. A well-loved face grows more beautiful in your memory; it never grows old. Spring never dies; the flowers never fade; the sky is always blue, and the sun bright gold. The things you have once seen are in your memory for always, and they grow more precious with the years. Even if your eyes no longer see, your heart never forgets."

9

He paused for a moment, as if recalling pictures out of the past. Then he went on:

"Losing your sight gives you a keener appreciation of the senses left to you. Music seems even more beautiful; voices you've loved are clearer; the fragrance of a rose is a keener delight than it ever was when you could both see and smell it. Life, my dear, even without sight, is a glorious adventure. Try always to remember that – won't you?"

"I'll try."

Professor Hartley nodded. "I am deeply grateful that I did not lose my sight until I was well on in years. I have the memory of the things of beauty to store in my mind. Peter has many years of usefulness and happiness ahead."

"Happiness!" Betsy's voice scorned the word.

"Yes – happiness," the old man repeated. "Never forget that, Betsy. It will be hard for Peter at first; he's young, unreconciled, bitter. It's only natural that he should be. He's going to need cheerful companionship, friendliness – but don't try to give him more than he is ready to take. Don't try to make him lean on you. Help him to be self-reliant, to live a normal life."

"I'll try," she repeated.

The old man smiled and patted her hand. "That's all anybody can do, Betsy," he told her.

Chapter Two

Centerville was a town of about five thousand; peaceful, pleasant, moving slowly in its placid days and nights. The center of a rich farming country, it boasted a small but prosperous textile mill and a few minor industries.

There was the usual Main Street, with four "business blocks" facing one another across a small green square where the inevitable war memorial stood guard.

George Drummond, Betsy's father, had inherited his father's law practice and offices, and the big white house on a pleasant street within walking distance of the business center.

Edith was in her early forties. She was brown-haired, brown-eyed, always neatly and becomingly dressed, and was what the town called admiringly "a good manager." George was three years older, his hair reddish, his eyes blue and friendly. Both were enormously popular in the little town and always spoken of as representative citizens.

George always walked home to lunch, and today, as he came near the gate set in the picket fence, he saw Betsy coming from the opposite direction. He stopped to wait for her, a warm glow about his heart, as there always was at the sight of her. For days he had known of her mental agony and grief – a grief which the whole town sincerely shared in the knowledge that one of its most popular young men had come out of the war hopelessly blind.

Betsy saw her father at the gate and flung up her hand in salute. But the unhappy look was still in her eyes. He dropped his arm about her shoulders and they went side by side up the walk, bordered on either side by tall tulips and hyacinths and bright yellow daffodils dancing in the soft spring wind.

"My, but you're a busy little gad-about," George teased. "Just getting home to lunch – and here your old man's put in a hard day already!"

"I went out to see Professor Hartley," Betsy told him. "He's training a pup for me."

"Training a pup? For what, if I may ask?"

Betsy's teeth touched her lower lip, but she made herself answer him steadily.

"You know he has one of the Seeing Eye dogs from that place in New Jersey – well,

13

there's a pup that he's training for me, to give Pete when he comes home." She blurted it all out in a single sentence, as though she dared not stop lest she be unable to go on.

"Oh, I see. Well, that's a pretty fine thing for Hartley to do – and you, too. Crazy as you are about pups, Pete ought to appreciate your giving him one instead of keeping it yourself."

"I don't need this one, and Pete does," she said, running ahead up the steps and into the house.

When George came into the dining room, she was already at the table, and Edith was talking with her. Betsy told of her encounter with Marcia.

"So, the old Cunningham place has been sold!" mused George, puzzled. "Funny I didn't hear anything about it. Usually a real estate sale creates quite a bit of excitement in town."

"I don't think she's bought the place, Pops," said Betsy. "She told me she had rented it for a year – and she was going to live here. Then she looked funny and said, 'If you can call it *living*'!"

Betsy ate hurriedly and went up to her room. Her father sat silent beside Edith whose mouth trembled a little as she spoke.

14

"Oh, George, what are we going to do about her?" she asked.

"I don't know, darling. I just don't know. It's the shock of young Marshall being blinded, of course."

Edith nodded. "She has a very bad attack of hero worship. You know how she trailed him before he went away. She wrote to him almost every day, and – well, she's grown up a bit – "

George resented that. "Grown up? She's only a baby! Why, she's only eighteen!"

"She'll be nineteen in six more months, darling." Edith's smile was warm, even if it did nothing to remove the anxiety from her eyes. "Girls today grow up terribly fast."

For a little while they were silent and, when they rose from the table, George put his arm about Edith's shoulders as she walked to the door with him.

When he had gone, she sighed and turned toward the stairs. She was not consciously walking softly. It was just that the stairs were carpeted and she wore thin-soled slippers. It did not occur to her to knock at Betsy's closed door. She simply turned the knob and pushed it open. She paused on the threshold, appalled at what she saw.

Betsy, a thick black bandage tied tightly about her eyes, was feeling her way

15

cautiously about the room. She was so absorbed in what she was doing that she was not aware that the door had opened until she heard her mother's exclamation of surprise.

Betsy whirled and tugged at the bandage, but she had knotted it so tightly that it would not come off easily. When it did, she faced her mother, flushed and angry.

"I didn't hear you knock, Mother."

Edith ignored that. "What is all this, Betsy?" she demanded. "Some idiotic game?"

"I don't suppose I could possibly hope to keep a secret in a family where I am treated like an infant in arms," Betsy burst out. "I can't see that it's anybody's business if I try to – to understand something about what it means to be blind."

Edith felt a little chill, and before she could stop herself she was saying sharply, "Betsy, this is utterly morbid! I won't have it, do you hear? It's a terrible thing that has happened to Peter Marshall, but it has happened to a great many fine young men all over the country. We simply have to face it and make the best of it."

"*We* have to make the best of it?" There was something very near contempt in Betsy's voice.

"I don't understand you any more," Edith

16

confessed, helplessly. "You were never engaged to Peter. Why, you were just a youngster when he went away."

"I've been in love with him since I was twelve years old," Betsy stated flatly, giving her mother a look that was almost hostile. "And I'll be in love with him until the day I die!" The young voice shook with such a passionate intensity that Edith was taken aback.

"Has he ever asked you to marry him?" she probed.

"Oh, no. He doesn't even know I'm in love with him. And I'm pretty sure he's not in love with me. But that's not important."

No amount of argument or cajoling could swerve her from that stand. When at last Edith had to admit defeat, she felt as though she had suffered a physical beating. She was sore and bruised and a little frightened.

Always, to Edith, her garden was a refuge when things got unpleasant. An hour of weeding, of transplanting, of planning, or spraying – anything that she could do in her garden – gave her comfort.

She went down the steps to the garden at last. But it was a long time before the warmth

17

of the spring sun, the moist dark earth that crumbled between her fingers and the tiny slips she was transplanting, could lay any sort of soothing peace over her troubled spirit.

Chapter Three

Edith called on Marcia Eldon a few days later. To her surprise, when she suggested that Betsy might like to go with her, Betsy agreed, as listlessly as she agreed to anything these days, seeming to find it an effort to keep her thoughts on anything save Peter Marshall.

Marcia ushered them into the dark old-fashioned living room. A more depressing room, Edith told herself, thinking fondly of her own flowered chintz draperies and light-colored furniture, she had seldom seen. She shuddered a little.

"I don't blame you. It *is* a chamber of horrors, isn't it?" said Marcia Eldon.

Edith said, "You've met Betsy, my daughter?"

"Oh, Betsy and I have met, haven't we? Do sit down – if you can stand this ghastly place," said Marcia, and dropped into a chair.

She wore yellow flannel slacks, superbly tailored, and a jade-green shirt. Her feet stockingless, were encased in high-heeled, gaily striped, sandals. Her shining black hair was loose about her shoulders, parted low at the side and swept back.

She drew a cigarette case out of her shirt pocket, offered it to Edith who declined and to Betsy who shook her head.

Marcia's eyebrows went up. "You don't smoke?"

"Silly, I know," admitted Edith, abashed. "But I just don't care for the taste. Betsy tried it and didn't like it, and – well, I know it makes us sound like something out a mid-Victorian opus–"

Marcia lit a cigarette. "Well," she said, "what shall we talk about?"

Edith flushed. "I merely came to tell you that I'm very glad the old house is being opened, and that I hope you'll be very happy in Centerville."

"Thanks, but I don't expect to be," Marcia announced coolly. "I expect nothing but to be bored to fits of screaming mi-mi's. But I'm sentenced to a year here so – " She lifted her shoulders in a little shrug.

Edith stiffened at this affront to her civic pride, which held firmly to the theory that Centerville was the best of all places to live.

"I'm sorry you feel that a year in Centerville is equal to a prison sentence,

Mrs. Eldon," she said. "I'm surprised you would come here, feeling that way."

Marcia's smile was lazy, but not unfriendly.

"I had no choice in the matter. I *had* to find a quiet place where I could live inexpensively. When Lucy Cunningham offered me this old barn, rent free for a year, what else could I do?"

Edith hid a natural and lively curiosity.

"How is Lucy, by the way? I haven't seen her in years," she said. "I was always fond of Lucy."

Marcia's smile was one of secret amusement.

"Then it's obvious you haven't seen Lucy recently," she drawled. "She's making a perfect fool of herself, throwing money away with both hands, sponsoring a lot of cheap little 'hangers-on' who profess artistic ambitions but are simply allergic to honest work."

Edith's eyes flashed, but before she could speak Marcia lifted a long, maroon-nailed hand and said, "Sorry. That sounds pretty low of me, when I am one of Lucy's 'hangers-on' and quite glad of a chance to sponge off her, doesn't it? But then, I really *am* an artist. I can pay back all that Lucy has given me, which is a lot more than any of the others will ever be able to do."

"Oh," said Edith politely. "You paint?"

"I'm a singer," returned Marcia. "And a very good one with a great deal of promise. I'm heading for opera – for a little while, anyway, until I can establish a name that will make it possible for me to demand good fees for concerts. I was fool enough to play too hard, and work too hard, and I ran into a bout with pneumonia that left my throat in bad shape. I have to take a year off. If I'm a good girl, eat my spinach, cut out late hour, liquor and fun, get ten hours sleep every night, my voice will be as good as new within a year – or else I'm going to murder my doctor for accepting money under false pretenses."

"I see," said Edith, merely to be polite, because she didn't see at all. There were depths to this girl she had not suspected; depths she wasn't at all sure she liked. Marcia Eldon seemed hard, callous, completely self-centered.

Marcia roused herself a little and remembered to be a hostess.

"Shall we have tea? Or would you prefer cocktails?" she suggested.

"Neither, thank you. I'm afraid we must

22

be going." Edith stood up. "Betsy and I just dropped in to welcome you to Centerville."

"Thanks," said Marcia. She glanced at Betsy and grinned as though they shared a secret that was a bit off-color, and walked with them to the door. As they went down the walk, Edith burst out impulsively:

"I don't think I like Mrs. Eldon."

Betsy laughed. "You know something? I don't think she gives a darn whether we like her or not."

"I can't think why Lucy gave her the house."

"Who is this Lucy-person?" asked Betsy. "All I ever knew was that this was the Cunningham place and none of the Cunninghams had lived here in years."

"Lucy is the daughter of the man who built the textile mills here. The family lived here for several generations," Edith explained. "Practically all of Centerville is built on what was once the old Cunningham plantation. There were thousands of acres of it – it dated back to a King's Grant given to one of the Oglethorpe settlers back in the 1700's."

Betsy nodded, pretending an interest she did not feel.

"Gone-with-the-Wind stuff, huh?" she suggested idly. "Living in a dump like that would sour Pollyanna's disposition. No wonder the Eldon lady is going sour."

"The Cunningham fortune was quite ample," Edith went on to explain, "and the old man invested it shrewdly. Finally, there was only Lucy to inherit it, when her brother was killed on a hunting trip. Lucy, poor dear, was a homely creature and she had a bad persecution complex. She thought the town made fun of her behind her back; she could never be friendly or at ease with any of the young men who would have been glad to marry her if only for her money. So when she came of age and the estate passed into her hands, she shook the dust of Centerville from her feet and went to New York, London, Paris and Antibes!"

"Good for Lucy," said Betsy. She thrust her hand through her mother's arm and said, ending the subject, "And now, let's have a soda, maybe do some shopping, and walk the old man home."

As she steered her mother toward the town's favorite drugstore, which was always crowded at this time of the day, Edith protested futilely, "Don't call your father 'the old man'! It's not respectful."

Betsy grinned. "He loves it," she said, and Edith knew it was true. Before she could manage an answer, Molly Prior hailed her

24

from a table near the front of the drug-store.

"Hello, Edith. The small fry's clamoring for your child, so come over and be your age. We're just dishing up a fresh patch of dirt," called Molly.

Betsy went on to a booth at the back of the room, while another chair was crowded into Molly Prior's table.

Edith's eyes followed Betsy, as she joined the "gang." There were almost a dozen boys and girls Betsy's age – the "high school set," they called themselves. Edith's heart eased a little as she saw the welcome they gave Betsy; the way the boys fell over themselves to make room for her.

"You're not listening, Edith! We are tearing the Eldon creature to bits," said Molly.

Edith looked around at her friends. "Mrs. Eldon, at the Cunningham place?" she queried. "How could you possibly know enough about her to talk about her? I've just come from there. Betsy and I called on her," Edith explained.

"What's she like?" demanded Anne Hutchens, a pretty, plump blonde whose maternity gown proclaimed her, as she proudly boasted, "a lady-in-waiting."

"Why, she's beautiful and very sophisticated looking – " Edith hesitated.

Molly interrupted, shaking her dark head so that the absurd earrings she wore shook against her cheek.

"I don't like her, either," she said. "She's definitely a menace and I, for one, intend to keep my husband under lock and key while she's in town."

The others laughed, knowing Tom Prior's devotion to his wife and her frank adoration of him.

"I'm so afraid both you and Tom will get pretty tired of that," said Edith. "She plans to be here a year. She told me so."

The others looked startled.

Chapter Four

Betsy awoke that morning and lay still for a long time, as consciousness began to sweep through her. Something important was going to happen today, an event that might change her whole life. And then, as she came fully awake, the realization crashed upon her.

Pete was coming home today.

Her body tensed beneath the thin covers and her hands tightened into fists. There was a frightened look in her eyes. The day she had dreamed of, and planned for so long, was here. All the happy, ecstatic dreams of seeing Pete, tall and strong and disturbingly attractive, swinging down the train steps and gathering her into his arms, his eyes devouring her. . . .

"His *eyes!*" she said, half aloud, as she swung out of bed.

Her breath caught on a sob and, for a moment, she put her hands over her own eyes, almost hating them for their clear sight. If only she could give them to Pete!

His train was due at ten o'clock. She got under the shower, towelled herself

27

vigorously, and reached into the closet for the cherished frock she had guarded so jealously for Pete's homecoming. But even as she touched the crisp pink pique, with the white buttons marching down the front, the little white cupcake of a hat, the brown and white sports pumps, she drew back, and once more her heart was twisted with pain.

She had yearned for the moment when she could stand before Pete, in all the glory of being grown-up, and see the look of delighted surprise in his eyes. His letters had told her that he still thought of her as a long-legged, coltish brat with braces on her teeth and carrot-colored hair. He wouldn't know that her hair had darkened until now she wore pink and it was vastly becoming. He wouldn't know that her skin was clear and fresh, faintly tinged with a very becoming tan. Pete wouldn't know anything about her. And suddenly it seemed to her an unbearable thing that to him she would always be just an awkward, freckle-faced child.

No, it wouldn't matter to Pete what she wore. Shorts, slacks, a peasant-dirndl such as she wore for every-day around the house, a party frock all white and silver and buoyant above small silver slippers – whatever she wore, however she looked, she would always be to Pete a kid in a gingham play suit. . . .

Her mother's voice called up to her:

"Betsy, aren't you ever coming down for breakfast?"

"Be right with you," she called back, trying hard to sound gay and casual.

She got into a blue and white print dress left over from last summer. It had faded a bit in the wash, and was one of the cotton dresses she kept for work in the garden, or when she was "playing around" with the gang on pursuits that did not require formal dressing. She brushed her hair back carelessly, made a face at herself in the mirror, and went down the stairs.

George, standing with Edith at the door, was leaving for the office. He grinned at Betsy.

"Hi, chum," he greeted her. "You look about ten years old."

She tried to smile at him, muttered something, and went into the dining room. Edith and George exchanged anxious glances.

"Oh, how I've dreaded this day!" Edith confessed.

George nodded. "I know. Thank the Lord it's only twelve hours long. His train gets in at ten?"

"Yes. Mrs. Marshall said he'd rather not be met with a reception committee or anything, that he just wanted to come home as though he'd been away for a short trip. I guess his nerves are pretty well banged up," said Edith.

"Then the kid won't be there?" asked George hopefully.

"Nothing short of a broken neck could keep her home."

George sighed; then he kissed the top of Edith's head and said, trying hard to be gay, "Well, we'll have to look on this as a sickness. We pulled her through typhoid, remember? And double whooping cough, and a few less serious childhood ailments. I guess we can see her through this."

"I hope so," said Edith, and managed to send him away with a smile.

She watched until he turned to wave to her, and then, the morning ritual complete, she went back to the dining room. Betsy was pushing one of Edith's nut-brown waffles about on her plate.

"What's the matter with that waffle?" Edith asked.

"Don't be a dope. Nothing's the matter with it. It's super – same as always," answered Betsy abstractedly.

"Then eat it, darling, while I fix you another one."

"Oh, for Pete's sake –" Betsy caught her

breath and paled a little. Secretly, she had always enjoyed the absurd expression which her world accepted simply as a mild expletive, but which, to her, always held a romantic flavor. She avoided her mother's eyes and went on, "I'm getting too fat in all the wrong places. Waffles have calories, or something. I've got to diet."

"I never heard such a silly statement. You're as skinny as a rail. Honey, you make me laugh!"

"Well, go ahead and laugh," Betsy flared. "But I still don't have to eat the darned waffle!"

She pushed back her chair and stood up. She muttered something, and was gone, running up the stairs to her room. Edith still sat at the table, her face white and tired.

A little later, as Betsy came downstairs, still wearing the faded blue and white cotton dress, Edith said:

"Aren't you going to the station to meet Peter?"

"Of course," returned Betsy curtly.

"You haven't much time to dress."

"I *am* dressed. What difference does it make what I wear or how I look?" Betsy burst out. "Pete won't know the difference."

And then she was gone, hurrying out

31

through the open door and down the walk before Edith could speak. . . .

There was always a little group of loafers around the station, as in all small towns where the daily passing of big-city trains is an event. Betsy ignored them as she paced the platform, straining her eyes along the track for the first sign of smoke that would herald the approach of the train bringing Peter.

A few minutes before train-time, a neat dark green sedan stopped at the edge of the station yard. Mrs. Marshall, trim and smart in her suit of printed silk, a hat made mostly of white violets perched becomingly on her carefully waved hair, got out. As she came along the platform, she was pulling on white gloves and there was a cluster of white violets pinned to her jacket.

Watching her, Betsy suddenly felt frowsy, in her last summer's cotton dress, her mahogany colored curls guiltless of a hat, socks and scuffed saddle-shoes on her feet. She flushed as she went to meet Mrs. Marshall, who greeted her affectionately and carefully veiled her look of disapproval.

"Well, Betsy, our long wait is over. Our boy is coming home. Won't it be grand to see him again?"

"It would be even grander if he could see

us," muttered Betsy, and caught her lower lip hard between her teeth.

"Betsy, you must pull yourself together." Mrs. Marshall said it quietly, but there was a note of sternness in her voice. "We've got to treat Pete exactly as though nothing has happened. We mustn't break down. He needs our comfort and our cheer – not our tears!"

Betsy tossed her head and said huskily, "Of course –" But her words were cut off by the sound of a train whistle.

Far up the line, where the railroad tracks seemed to run together, there was smoke, and then the train came rushing in. Betsy clenched her hands tightly, and held her breath. Mrs. Marshall gave her a glance that was almost hostile, and then turned as the train slid to a halt.

Mrs. Marshall walked a few steps away from Betsy, who stood as though rooted to the spot. The conductor swung down and a young man appeared at the top of the steps – a tall young man much thinner than Betsy had been prepared to see. He was still in uniform, with the bars of a lieutenant on his shoulder, and his thin face seemed paler because of the dark glasses that shielded his eyes.

"Hello, there, son!" Mrs. Marshall called out.

Her cry seemed to Betsy to be unbearably gay, but the young man's face brightened. He seemed unaware of the conductor's gentle touch that guided him as he stepped down to the platform, and caught his mother in his arms.

"Home at last, Mom. It's swell to see you!" Peter's voice rang with such boyish delight that Betsy could scarcely keep back the tears.

They clung together for a long moment. Mrs. Marshall smiled at Peter, though her face was white and taut.

Still clinging to his hand, she said – and Betsy marvelled at her poise – "There's someone else here to greet you, darling."

"Oh, Mom, not a committee!" Peter groaned. "You promised – "

"A committee of two, darling. Just Betsy and me." Mrs. Marshall turned to Betsy, a stern command in her eyes.

"Betsy!" Peter grinned and held out his hand. "Betsy, you nice kid! This makes coming home perfect."

It was then that Betsy disgraced herself, in her own eyes, as well as in Mrs. Marshall's. She gave a little choked cry of heart break and jerked her hand free of

Peter's. Then she ran blindly along the platform and into the street – away from that tall, white-faced boy with his shadowed, sightless eyes.

Behind her, Mrs. Marshall ground her teeth in anger, as Peter's face went taut and his jaw clamped hard.

"Sorry – I seem to have upset the kid," said Peter.

"The car's over here, dearest," said Mrs. Marshall, knowing that there was no way in which she could see the hurt that Betsy's outbreak had caused him. She slipped her hands through his arm and, without seeming to guide him, drew him toward the car.

The station loafers, who had witnessed Betsy's outburst, shuffled embarrassedly, and several of them called to Peter. Then the station master came out to shake his hand and to say, "Glad to have you back, Pete. The whole town's mighty proud of you. Don't reckon they're gonna forgive you, though, for not letting 'em meet you with a brass band and a welcoming committee."

Peter managed a laugh as he shook hands with the man, and answered, "Hate to upset the town, but I'm not quite up to brass bands just yet. Give me a few days to get settled, and we'll whoop her up."

"Sure, sure, Pete. I just wanted you to

know how everybody feels about you, boy
– and that's mighty proud!" said the station
master.

Mrs. Marshall was eternally grateful to
him that he made no effort to assist Peter as
he climbed into the sedan. She got in behind
the wheel and, though her hand shook a little
as she switched on the ignition, she was
chattering almost hysterically, and the sound
of her voice hid the small jangling of the
keys.

Peter relaxed as the car started. After a
moment he put his hand on hers, and said,
"Okay, Mom – thanks! You can cut the act
now."

Mrs. Marshall managed to stifle the sob
that rose in her throat, and to say brightly,
"I don't know what you're talking about. I
never put on acts, and you know it. If I'm so
glad to see you that I have trouble to keep
from exploding, is that so strange?"

"Of course not, pet!" Peter smiled at her.
"I know it was a sock in the jaw to see me.
I waited as long as I could, so you could get
used to the idea of seeing me like this. I knew
it would be a bitter blow."

"Peter Marshall, you talk like a fool! Don't
you suppose I'm tickled silly to see you, with
your arms and legs intact? Every mother who
saw her son go off to war braced herself for

36

the worst that would possibly happen to him! I'm lucky that you came back at all!"

Peter grinned and relaxed a little.

"Atta girl, Mom!" he said, and Mrs. Marshall breathed a little more easily.

All along the street as she wound her way through the mid-morning traffic, people called to them, waved, and shouted greetings to Peter. Peter smiled and waved back. When they reached the house and his mother had stopped the car at the steps, he grinned and sniffed.

"Boy, oh, boy, it *smells* like home! You'll never know what it's like to smell clean, decent odors again – flowers and new-cut grass and freshly plowed fields –" He broke off to sniff again.

Mrs. Marshall laughed, and refrained from helping him as he got out of the car and, with his stick, probed a little until he got his bearings. He went up the steps aided only by the cane; he swung open the screen door for her; the tip of his cane touched the door sill, and he followed her into the house.

Chapter Five

Late that afternoon Betsy took a bus out to Professor Hartley's cottage. She knew he would be in the garden at the back of the house today, and she went around there. As always, he sat up alertly in his big rustic chair as he heard the sound of her footsteps on the gravel.

"Hello, Betsy, my dear," he greeted her. "You are all dressed up."

Betsy stared at him. "But, how did you know that?"

He chuckled, enjoying the surprise in her voice.

"High-heeled slippers make an entirely different sound, on gravel, from that of low-heeled oxfords, my dear," he reminded her. "Also, there's a very faint whispering that sounds as though it might be – oh, silk, or perhaps thin starched material – "

"It's pale pink pique," she told him, "and it's very becoming. I've got a hat that looks like a slightly over-sized magnolia – and I look very nice."

38

The fact that her gaiety wobbled a little, did not escape the old man.

"And you've been crying," he said.

Betsy caught her breath. "Pete's home," she said unsteadily.

The old man nodded, his sightless eyes upon her as though he could read her young face.

"And you broke down and cried when you saw him?" There was gentle censure in his voice.

Her face crumpled and she drew a deep, hard breath. "Yes," she admitted. "And I'm ashamed. But I couldn't help it."

"That's bad, Betsy. I'm disappointed in you."

"He still thinks I'm a child," she said, sullenly.

There was gentle, but genuine amusement in the old man's smile.

"And why shouldn't he think that, Betsy? Have you ever behaved in a grown-up manner with him?" he suggested.

A burning flush crept over Betsy's face and her eyes dropped, as though he could read their expression.

"No, of course not," she stammered, resentfully. "When he went away, I *was* just a kid. And today – well today, he couldn't tell the difference!"

He nodded. "But now he's home, and that's a challenge to you, Betsy," he pointed out. "Are you going to face that challenge with as much courage as he has?"

She was silent for a while, her hands clenched together in the lap of the cherished pink pique.

"Can I take Gus to see him?" she asked presently.

"I don't know. *Can* you?"

Betsy flushed. "I meant – *may* I?"

"And I meant – *can* you?"

"Sure," said Betsy. "I get you. You mean, can I take it? Can I walk in on Pete and be gay and nonchalant?"

"That was what I meant."

Betsy stood up, smoothed down the pink pique with a loving hand, and thrust her young chin out belligerently.

"Sure I can," she said. "Watch me."

She whistled and the two dogs came bounding to her, leaping about her with obvious pleasure. She bent and caressed the older dog, and then she snapped the leather leash on the collar of the younger dog, who gave a little excited yip at this indication that he was about to be taken for a walk.

"Good luck, Betsy," said the professor.

"Thanks. I'll report in the morning."

"Do that. I'll be anxious."

40

Betsy turned with a whirl of the pink pique.

"You needn't be. Your pep-talk really got me! I'll pick up the challenge, and everything will be fine."

"Of course."

Betsy went away, the dog trotting along beside her, his handsome head erect, on his very best behavior.

Betsy was glad that she had to walk back to the Marshall place. It was almost a mile from Professor Hartley's, and the day was unseasonably warm. But she was oblivious to the heat; she didn't even know that her forehead was wet with perspiration or that the pique dress was getting a trifle limp.

The door stood open, the screen unlatched. But before she could open the screen door, she saw Mrs. Marshall standing there. Her heart quailed a little at the expression on the woman's face.

"Oh, hello," said Betsy uneasily.

Mrs. Marshall held open the door saying, "Come in, Betsy."

"I was looking for Pete," said Betsy. "I've brought him a present."

She indicated the dog, whose golden eyes were fastened appraisingly on Mrs. Marshall, as if trying to decide whether she was friend or foe.

"Oh, what a beautiful dog! Peter will love him!" Mrs. Marshall put a hand out experimentally for the dog to sniff it before she touched him.

"I'm sorry about this morning," Betsy began.

Mrs. Marshall straightened and her eyes were cold.

"You should be, Betsy," she said. "After all the talks we've had, after our plans that nothing was to upset Peter – "

"I – it sort of hit me all of a heap," Betsy confessed humbly.

Mrs. Marshall's face softened a little.

"But we have to help him, Betsy, not drown him in a sea of tears and pity."

Betsy nodded miserably. "I know. I've just been given a good going-over by Professor Hartley. He was plenty tough, so you needn't bother to add anything to it. He hits hard, but he hits straight."

"He's a wonderful person," Mrs. Marshall said quietly.

Betsy managed to raise her eyes to Mrs. Marshall's. "Could I see Pete, and introduce him to Gus?"

Mrs. Marshall hesitated. "No tears? No emotional outbursts? Promise?"

Betsy lifted a finger and crossed her heart, solemnly, like a penitent child.

Mrs. Marshall smiled. "He's out in the garden. But, so help me, Betsy," she added, "if you upset him again, I'll wring your neck with my bare hands."

"I hope you do, Mrs. Marshall," said Betsy simply.

Betsy saw, as she came around the house, a tall figure lying in one of the long canvas beach chairs. For a moment she was still, and the dog, puzzled, tugged at the leash and stirred uneasily.

Betsy made herself go forward, her heels clicking softly on the flagstone path. She saw Peter tense a little and his head go up. The thin face, its cheekbones standing out too prominently, turned toward her, and the sunlight glinted on the dark glasses.

"Hello?" said Peter, his voice hesitant. Obviously he was not sure who it was, and was a little embarrassed by that fact.

Betsy made her voice sound gay and casual, as she went forward, saying, "Hello, Pete! It's swell having you home again."

"Betsy!" said Pete. Then he drew back, his jaw setting. "Think you can overcome your repulsion long enough to shake hands with a misfit?"

Her voice caught in a little sob, but she made herself say, "Don't be a dope, you dope! I was so glad to see you this morning

43

that the only way I could keep from flinging myself into your arms was to run out on you. After all, a girl's got to have a little pride."

It was not too convincing, but it was the best she could do.

"And since when has it been a scandalous business for you to fling yourself in my arms, Betsy? After all, you did that when I left – remember? There was quite a gang at the station, too!" Peter's voice was a trifle on the grim side.

"Oh, but I'm a big girl now," Betsy told him airily, her eyes pleading for his understanding.

"You're a long-legged, carrot-topped, big-eyed brat with braces on your teeth – " began Peter, and some of the tension had gone out of his voice.

"I am not!" she flashed. "I haven't got braces on my teeth, and I'm not a carrot-top – " Suddenly her voice died in her throat, because always Peter would see her, behind the blindness, as just that! Peter couldn't ever know she had grown up, or that she was no longer a homely kid. "I'm – well, I'm *pretty* now," she announced.

Peter grinned. "Modest aren't you?" he teased.

"Well, I have to tell you – otherwise you wouldn't know," she defended herself, and

44

rushed on impulsively, "I didn't send you a picture, Pete. I sort of wanted to burst on you in all my glory." Her voice stuck again.

Peter laughed, but there was a faint edge to his voice and Betsy saw that his hand had tightened a little on the chair arm.

"And then, when I came back, I couldn't see you. So you had to tell me," he finished for her.

"Well," she protested youthfully, "I *am* pretty. People think so, anyway! My hair's not red any more. It's sort of mahogany-colored; and it curls – remember? And I've grown two inches, and I'm nineteen! I'm too old to run around kissing young men who've just come back from the war – in public, anyway!"

"Especially young men who come back all crocked up, eh, Bets?"

Betsy walked deliberately over to him, framed his face between her small brown hands, unconscious that they were shaking. She tilted his face back a little, bent her head and set her young mouth warmly on his. . . .

Peter pushed her away from him, and said bitterly, "Cut! A very nice scene, my dear, but I'm not having any! Your lovely sacrifice to a 'wounded hero' is appreciated, but declined with thanks!"

"I love you, Peter," said Betsy, simply.

45

For a moment Peter was still. Then he sprang to his feet and said almost violently, "Cut it, Betsy! Behave yourself! You've been to the movies again. You aren't in love with me. Now run along home and call your boy-friend."

Betsy flinched as though he had struck her. As she drew back a step, involuntarily, she brushed against the waiting dog, watching the little scene uneasily, disturbed by the raised voices of this strange man and the girl he, Gus, had come to know as a friend.

"Oh," said Betsy, bitterly humiliated yet anxious to get things back on a friendly basis, "I almost forgot. I brought you a present."

She led Gus over to stand beside Peter.

"Thanks –" Peter began roughly, but when he felt the warmth of the dog's body against his leg, put down an investigating hand. "Good gosh, a dog!" he said, as Gus sniffed his hand doubtfully.

"And he's beautiful, Pete. He's a German shepherd, and so intelligent he really ought to have a college degree. Professor Hartley trained him for you – like the Seeing Eye dogs, you know!"

Peter withdrew his hand from the dog's head, his face white and set.

"Oh, a Seeing Eye dog, eh? Where's the
46

tin cup and lead pencils?" he asked. "Or must I supply those myself?"

Betsy stood quite still in front of him, looking at him with wide hurt eyes.

"You don't like Gus?" she whispered. "Oh, Pete, he's beautiful. And he's been yours since the day he was born. Professor Hartley thought you'd like him."

The pain and humiliation in her tone cut straight at Peter, and he said, "Cut the tears, Betsy. Sure, he's a swell dog. We'll have fun together. Thanks a lot."

"I'll take him away."

"Don't, Betsy."

Her young head was high. "He's much too nice a dog to be left somewhere where people don't want him," she announced hotly. "He loves me, and I'll take him home with me!"

"I'm sorry, Betsy." The anger was gone from Peter's voice now, and there was a trace of compunction there. "I'll be glad to have him. I've always wanted a good dog. Gus and I will have a swell time together. Thanks a million!"

Betsy hesitated. It was hard to tell what a man was really thinking unless you could see his eyes. But it seemed incredible that Peter could not want Gus.

"Here's his leash." She put the leather loop in Peter's hand. "Of course, he's got a wooden harness, too. That fastens to his collar, and you hold it when you walk with him, so he can guide you."

Once more bitterness twisted Peter's face. "Sure, I know. And then the dog puts in the rest of his life keeping a useless hulk from dashing his brains out at street crossings and the like. A heck of a life for a dog – just because a guy can't get around by himself."

"I'm sorry, Peter. I thought you'd like him. I knew if you really wanted a Seeing Eye dog, you could go to Morristown, and they'd give you one and help you train him – and it would only cost you a dollar, because you're a service man. Only – well, I sort of thought that if it was one that somebody *liked* you well enough to raise and train for you –"

"How old is he?"

"Eight months old."

"How long has the training been going on?"

"Five months and six days."

"Since the day Mom knew about me?"

"Of course."

"I'm sorry, Betsy. I blew up, I guess. You and the professor are tops. I'm grateful, honestly, and I'll take good care of Gus."

"He'll want to take care of you," she pointed out. "That's his job. That's what he's been trained for."

48

"Well, I guess if that's what he wants, that's what he'll have to have," said Peter, and the iron band that had enclosed Betsy's heart loosened a little.

She dared not trust herself to stay longer for the tears were crowding close. So she knelt beside the uneasy dog, put her arms about him, and said, "Be a good egg, Gus, and look after him – hear?"

Before Peter could speak she was on her feet again, saying, "I've got to scoot for home now, or the folks will have a searching party out for me. 'Bye, Pete."

The dog moved to follow her, but she said, "Back, Gus! You stay here."

Gus whimpered a little, but dropped obediently to the grass beside Peter, and watched her go, with mournful, anxious eyes.

When the last click of her footsteps had gone, Peter dropped down into his chair. He put out his hand, feeling, until it encountered the dog's rough coat.

"Never mind, old boy," he said. "We both know you'd be a darned sight happier with her, but we can't go on kicking a kid in the teeth. You're her gift to me, and it would break her heart if we didn't make the best of it. But don't worry, old timer. You're going to be a *dog*, and not just a work-horse for a guy who's going to find his way around without your help! You can chase squirrels, and cats and have yourself a time! So take it easy, pal."

Gus kept his eyes fixed longingly in the direction Betsy had taken.

Chapter Six

Marcia Eldon had been accepted by Edith's friends, who were the town's most representative women. Accepted politely, if not too cordially. There were reservations on both sides. Marcia accepted their hospitality politely; they extended it cautiously. But after the first few occasions on which she had been – as they all knew, though no one admitted it publicly – on trial, the other women relaxed a little.

Marcia made no play for the attention of the men. She was friendly, but not unduly so. The men had been, at first, a little afraid of their wives, and not quite at ease with Marcia. But Marcia was obviously unimpressed to any great degree by any of them, and once the women saw that she played scrupulously fair with their husbands, the tension eased.

"She's a darned good-looking woman," admitted Molly Prior one afternoon when she and Edith were spending a lazy hour in Edith's garden. "I wonder how old she is."

"About twenty-seven, I imagine,"

answered Edith absently, gazing contentedly at the double row of snapdragons which she had transplanted a week ago and which were thriving.

"Nearer thirty, I'd say," said Molly. "I wonder whatever happened to Mr. Eldon."

Edith laughed. "I'm afraid that's something I wouldn't know. She's never mentioned him to me."

Marcia had kept her own counsel and, while the women invited her to their dinner parties at which the husbands were present, as well as to their "hen parties," they knew little more about her now than they had when she came to Centerville.

On the afternoon when Betsy had tried to make her peace with Peter, and had left her gift of the dog, Marcia was driving her gray coupe out toward the end of the city street. Seeing Betsy trudging along, her head down, her brown-toed slippers scuffing miserably at the dust, Marcia slowed the car and leaned out.

"Going my way?" she called.

Betsy flung up a startled head, and Marcia saw the glimmer of tears on her cheeks.

"I – no, thanks. I'm going home," stammered Betsy, and turned her head away.

"Then hop in and I'll drive you," invited Marcia, swinging open the door. "It's too hot to walk. Besides, I'm lonely. Be a good girl and join me in my miseries!"

Betsy lacked the strength or the composure to argue, so she climbed into the coupe and Marcia drove to the next corner and turned. Betsy sat huddled, her eyes straight ahead. Marcia glanced at her curiously.

"Want a shoulder to cry on?" she asked.

Betsy flinched, but said nothing.

"It's a man, of course."

Betsy flung her companion a defiant glance, but Marcia smiled and said:

"When a pretty girl walks along the street in tears, the answer is always a man."

"What's the good of being pretty when the only man you ever cared about can't see you?" Betsy demanded.

"Oh, I wouldn't worry about that, chick. First thing you know, he'll snap out of it and his eyes will be opened and – "

Betsy shivered. "He won't ever snap out of it. He's – he's blind," she whispered.

"Oh, you poor chick. I'm terribly sorry. I didn't dream it could be anything like that," said Marcia gently.

Betsy was struggling with tears, and as they turned into the street where they both lived, Marcia said impulsively, "Why don't you come and have dinner with me? It'll give

53

you a chance to pull yourself together before you have to face your parents."

"Thanks," said Betsy huskily.

Inside the house, Marcia gave her shoulder a friendly pat and said, "Run upstairs to my bedroom and pull yourself together. You'll find powder and things. Use whatever you need. I'll telephone your mother – all right?"

Betsy couldn't manage an answer, but she did manage a damp smile and fled gratefully up the old staircase.

When she came down a little later, she had washed her face in cold water, and had given herself a stern pep-talk. She was determined to be "very adult about the whole thing." It was the "gang's" favorite expression, and Betsy had decided that now was the time for her to put the expression into practice.

"Out here, chick," Marcia called.

Betsy followed the sound of Marcia's voice out to the old side-veranda, where honeysuckle and clematis vines made a fragrant curtain of white and cream-colored blossoms.

Marcia sat relaxed in a wicker chair. As Betsy came out, she smiled and motioned to another wicker chair, with broad arms and faded cushions.

"We're having dinner from trays out here

54

on the porch," she explained. "It's too hot in the house, and anyway, the house smothers me. I use it just to sleep in."

She was chattering on lightly, giving Betsy time to adjust herself. The smell of food did not, as Betsy anticipated, make her sick after all. Betsy was sniffing appreciatively of the fragrance that rose from her tray.

"Fall to," said Marcia, and dug a fork into the crisp salad.

Betsy began to eat and, gradually, as her empty stomach stopped protesting so much, she began to feel better. Marcia chatted lightly, amusingly, and finally she won the tribute of a small giggle from Betsy.

"There! You see? What you needed most of all was good food and light conversation," said Marcia, smiling.

"You're a pretty swell person, Mrs. Eldon."

"Not Mrs. Eldon, Betsy – in Heaven's name! My name is Marcia!"

"Thanks. I'll remember."

It was not until Marcia had removed the trays and was relaxed, a cigarette in her hand, that she looked at Betsy and said quietly:

"Want to talk about it? Or would you rather I just kept quiet?"

"It's something that can't be helped by talking. Pete has come home and he's blind."

55

"What a rotten shame! But the doctors are wonderful nowadays – " Marcia began.

Betsy shook her head. "No, it's completely hopeless. Pete's wonderful. He's – well, he's faced up to it, and is going to make the best of it. *I'm* the one that can't take it," she added, her chin quivering.

"It's harder for you, of course," Marcia said.

Betsy flung up her head. "Harder for me?" she repeated, incredulously.

Marcia nodded. "He has the – well, the challenge of a problem that will keep him fighting for a long time; all you can do is sit on the sidelines and watch – and cheer – and learn not to try to help him."

"That's what Professor Hartley said!"

"Great minds run in the same channel," Marcia commented, grinning. "Who is this Professor Hartley?"

"He used to be a college professor," answered Betsy. "And then he went blind. He's been blind for twenty years. The first five years he was so bitter about it that he just lay down and let it lick him. Then he snapped out of it and began to fight. And now – well, he's tops. He lives alone in a cottage at the end of town; he has a garden that he tends himself, all except the plowing;

56

and he does his own housework. He's marvelous."

"He sounds quite a person," answered Marcia. "This Pete – who is he?"

Betsy's eyes glowed and Marcia stared at her, touched with pity.

"Well, Pete's – it's a little hard to tell you," Betsy tried to explain. "I've known him since I was in rompers; I've been in love with him since I was twelve; he was seventeen then, and I bored the dickens out of him trailing him everywhere he went. I was a brat, I guess. My hair was carroty, I had braces on my teeth, and I was skinny and long-legged and pretty dumb – "

"Now he's come back, and you've grown into a very pretty girl and he doesn't know it," Marcia finished, with womanly insight.

"I guess that's pretty dumb of me," Betsy admitted.

"It isn't anything of the sort. It's perfectly natural. It's the way any normal girl would feel."

Betsy looked at her gratefully. "Thanks," she said.

Marcia was silent for a moment, and then she said casually, "I'd like to meet this boyfriend of yours. Do you think he'd care to have company?"

"I think so. Pete always liked people and

57

was more fun than anybody else in the gang."

"Well, we'll go out and see him then. Perhaps he'd like to go for a ride out in the country. We mustn't let him get lonely or bored," said Marcia.

"No, of course not."

And so a few afternoons later, Betsy and Marcia drove into the gravelled driveway at the big Marshall home. Marcia looked about her, her eyebrows lifting a little in surprise.

"So this is where your Pete lives," she murmured. "It's obvious that none of his troubles are financial."

"Oh, no, of course not."

"Well, anyway," murmured Marcia, "it's nice your Peter won't have to be bothered with earning his own living."

Mrs. Marshall, hearing the car, had come out on the veranda. Now she came down the steps, greeting Betsy pleasantly, saying cordially to Marcia, "How nice of you to call, Mrs. Eldon! Won't you come in? Or shall we go out in the garden? I believe it is cooler there."

"The garden, by all means, Mrs. Marshall," Marcia said. "What a lovely place you have here."

"Thank you."

Mrs. Marshall led the way along the

flagstoned walk to the garden, where Pete lay relaxed in a canvas beach chair, the dog, Gus, at his feet.

"I've brought you some company, darling," said Mrs. Marshall. "Here's Betsy – and Mrs. Eldon. Mrs. Eldon, may I present my son?"

"Hello, Betsy," said Peter. And to Marcia, "Delighted, Mrs. Eldon."

"Thank you." Marcia's voice was warm and sweet, with a faintly husky note that was very intriguing. Pete sat up a little and turned his sightless eyes, shielded by the dark glasses, toward her.

Betsy was busy greeting Gus, thankful that for the moment she did not have to speak. Pete knew her voice so well that one wrong note would tell him how hard it was to look at him, knowing he could never look at her, or at anything, so long as he lived.

They were served tall glasses of iced tea, sprigged with mint, dainty sandwiches, and frosted cakes still warm from the oven.

Marcia looked about the lovely old garden and sighed.

"How very fortunate you are, Mr. Marshall," she said.

Mrs. Marshall drew a sharp breath and Betsy looked up, white-faced and angry. But

Pete, his sightless eyes on Marcia, merely tensed a little.

"Yes, I *am* fortunate. I admit it – and I'm grateful," he said. It was as though he spoke to himself, as well as to those who sat about him.

"I knew you realized it," Marcia told him. "This lovely house, a beautiful garden, all the creature comforts – "

"While a heck of a lot of fellows in my position have nothing," finished Peter. "I know."

Marcia turned to Mrs. Marshall, who was looking at her with frightened eyes, and said lightly, "I was wondering, Mrs. Marshall, if you and Mr. Marshall could possibly endure an evening in the chamber of horrors? I'm asking you for dinner, if you can."

Peter laughed. "The chamber of horrors? That's the old Cunningham place where you're staying – a pretty apt description, at that!"

"It's very kind of you, Mrs. Eldon. We'd like it, I'm sure," said Mrs. Marshall.

Marcia laid a hand on the older woman's arm and said, "Please, won't you call me Marcia? 'Mrs. Eldon' makes me feel – oh, old and stiff and done with life! I can't afford a feeling like that, now that I'm losing a year out of my life, and I have so many things to do before I really *am* old."

"Losing a year out of your life?" Peter repeated, interested.

Marcia nodded, as though he could see her.

"I am going to be a good singer," she announced. "I have a very fine voice. But I made a fool of myself and overworked it. Now I have to take a year to rest up, and let my voice mend. I could have gone a long, long way this year, if I hadn't been a fool!"

She mentioned her voice and her future as casually, as frankly, as though she were speaking of some other person. There was no attitude of false modesty, no pretense of deprecation. She was obviously quite firm in her belief in her voice and its future.

"That's a rotten break," said Pete.

"We'll have to cheer each other up." Marcia smiled. "I've offended the town's best people by confessing that I look on my year in Centerville as little less than a prison sentence. I suppose it's an affront to their civic pride – just as though I wouldn't consider a year in Shangri-La a prison sentence, under the circumstances!"

She stood up to go. "Then I shall expect you for dinner – shall we say Thursday?" she said to Mrs. Marshall.

61

Pete echoed his mother's enthusiastic acceptance of the invitation and, as Marcia and Betsy drove away, Betsy said enviously:

"You made him laugh! And you've coaxed him to accept an invitation away from home. Nobody else has been able to do either of those things."

"That's because he's sorry for me."

Betsy stared at her. "Sorry for you?"

"And not sorry for himself, pet!" Marcia added. "That's the whole keynote of Pete's character. He can be sorry for others, but he's got too much courage to be sorry for himself! That's why he's - well, such a marvelous person."

"Are *you* telling *me?*" Betsy demanded, indignantly.

Marcia laughed. "I don't have to, do I?"

As she let Betsy out at the drive that led up to the Drummond house, Marcia said, "Of course, dear, you know I meant you are to come to dinner, too, on Thursday. You understood that, didn't you?"

Betsy's eyes brightened. "Well, no, I didn't. But I'd love to come. Thanks a lot."

Chapter Seven

When Betsy ran across the lawn and up the weed-grown drive to the Cunningham place on Thursday night, she was thinking of nothing but that in a few minutes now she would see Peter. But the little tight pain of the thought that was always just behind – that Peter would never see anybody or anything again – made her wince.

She was startled when she entered the ugly old living room to see that there was already a group of people there. Peter and his mother had not yet arrived, but two young men and two pretty girls perched about on the slippery horsehair furniture, and Marcia was passing a tray of cocktails.

"Oh, hello, Betsy. Come in," said Marcia. "I believe you know everybody, don't you?"

"Of course." Betsy exchanged greetings with Pauline Semmes, Anne Gray, Bobbie Prior and Steve Ellis. They were all several years older than she; Bobbie and Steve had been recently discharged from the service.

As Marcia took the cocktail tray to the kitchen, Betsy followed her, protesting in a low voice, "But, Marcia, I don't think Pete wants to see – I mean, to meet – people, yet."

"Then Peter is a very silly boy," said Marcia. "It's high time he was meeting people. It will be good for him; he can't crawl into a hole, and pull the hole in after him – not unless he wants to get warped and morbid. I invited Steve and Bobbie and their dates because they're just out of the Army, and veterans always like to trade experiences."

"Experiences!" exclaimed Betsy, furiously. "Bobbie Prior spent his eighteen months in this country, at a desk job; and Steve Ellis broke his foot in the first six months of basic training and never got closer to combat duty – "

"Is that their fault?" Marcia asked, and there was an edge to her voice. "You're being very silly. Shall we go back and join the others?"

Without waiting for an answer, Marcia pushed open the door and crossed the dining room to the living room, where the others were laughing and talking.

Betsy felt hot and uncomfortable. Marcia's curtness had surprised her and she was resentful. She was convinced that Pete would not have come to dinner tonight if he had

64

been told that there were going to be other guests.

When the sound of a car in the drive announced the arrival of Peter and his mother, Marcia went on talking to Bobbie Prior, although Betsy felt that she should have gone to the door to greet her guests. But the door stood open in the friendly, hospitable way that all doors stood open in Centerville throughout the summer, and a moment later Peter and his mother came into the hall.

Marcia met them at the doorway, and Peter's smile flashed warmly at her.

She slid her hand through his arm and steered him into the living room, saying, "I think you know everybody here – Pauline Semmes, Anne Gray, Bobbie Prior, and Steve Ellis."

Betsy held her breath, her eyes on Peter's face, ready to read the first flicker of an expression that would show her he hated coming face to face with people. Instead, she saw his face light up with a smile. She heard the warmth of his voice and saw the firmness with which he shook hands with the two men.

"I hear you've been to a war, fella!" said Bobbie cheerfully, and there was nothing in his voice to indicate the pity revealed in his eyes. "What was it like?"

Pete grinned. "Oh, not much fun. I've enjoyed other things more."

"So I can imagine," said Bobbie. "Tough luck, fella!"

"Oh, it could have been worse. At least I got back," said Peter, and Betsy felt tears dropping in her heart.

"Well, it wasn't much fun where I was, either," said Steve. Although his voice rang a little with a false gaiety, it was apparent that Peter was not too critical. "Of course, with the wound I got – "

"You were hit?" asked Pete.

Bobbie chuckled. "Don't start handing Steve any Purple Hearts. He tripped over his gun at maneuvers and broke his foot! He fought the battle of a military hospital. The only engagements he ever got tangled up in were with the pretty nurses!"

"Pay him no mind. The guy's jealous because he wasn't as smart as I was," said Steve, grinning.

"Have you ever seen this living room, Peter?" asked Marcia.

"No – they tell me it's something out of this world," answered Peter. Betsy, still watching him, thought she saw a tautness about his mouth.

66

"Well, it really should be seen to be believed," Marcia assured him, lightly casual. "But I'll do my best to describe it. Shall we go around?"

Deftly, she led him on a circuit of the room, describing each article they passed. Betsy, with a little catch at her heart, realized that Marcia was really mapping the room for Peter, so that he could steer his way about it, unaided, after this one circuit.

Mrs. Marshall, also watching them, whispered to Betsy, "She's a lovely person, isn't she?"

"She's grand," returned Betsy.

Throughout the simple but excellent dinner, Betsy was conscious of Marcia's unobtrusive manner of protecting Peter from any feeling of discomfort or embarrassment. Again she heard Peter laugh. She heard him talking with animation and humor to Bobbie and Steve and realized that they were trading experiences. The girls chimed in, with light laughter, because the stories related were amusing and care-free.

The whole evening was illuminating to Betsy. When Peter and Mrs. Marshall took their departure, the others following close behind, Betsy lingered to say, "Thanks, Marcia. You're swell!"

Marcia, emptying ash-trays and tidying the big ugly room looked at her, puzzled.

"That's sweet of you, dear," she said. "But is there any reason for the orchid?"

"Of course. You know there is. You were wonderful to Peter. He had fun. He – he *laughed!*" Betsy blinked back the tears.

"Why shouldn't he? After all, he's by no means the only man blinded in Vietnam, and he is very fortunate in having enough money not to have to earn a living. I suppose the Marshalls are very rich, aren't they?"

Betsy paused to think that over. Funny, but she had never stopped to consider whether or not the Marshalls were rich. Of course, they had the finest home in town; but after all, Centerville was a small town. Mrs. Marshall dressed smartly, but conservatively; there seemed to be plenty of money.

"Well, yes, I suppose they are," she said at last. "It's funny, but I'd never thought much about it."

Marcia was lightly derisive. "Oh, well, you probably wouldn't notice it, since your family has plenty," she answered carelessly. "I just thought Peter was very fortunate."

"I guess he is," Betsy admitted, though she didn't think so in her heart. Fortunate – when he was blind? When he would never again see the beauty he loved?

"You are very much in love with him, aren't you?"

Betsy frowned. "You've heard of the girl who wore her heart on her sleeve, so that everybody in the world knew who it belonged to? Well, her name is Betsy Drummond."

Marcia hesitated, and after a moment she said, "Betsy, don't you think you'd be much happier if you got over Peter, and found yourself another beau?"

"Got over Pete? Well, good grief, don't you suppose I would if I could? Do you think I *like* being in love with a man who can never know I'm anything but a long-legged, freckle-faced brat? Don't you suppose I'd rather find myself someone who could look at me and know I'm grown-up?" Betsy blurted out, struggling to hold back the tears. "But you can't turn love on and off like you would a water-faucet. I wish you could. Good night, Marcia, and thanks for the nice evening."

And she fled before the ignominious tears that threatened her.

For a while Marcia stood quite still, staring at the door through which Betsy had gone, her eyes inscrutable. Finally, she shrugged, and went about turning off the lights and making the house ready for the night. . . .

After that Thursday night Peter began to appear among his friends. It was as though, having braced himself and plunged into contact with other people, he found it easier to face them. It seemed, too, that the young people of Centerville had discovered Marcia and the strange charm that enveloped the old Cunningham house. Almost every evening there was a group on the old-fashioned veranda, behind the fragrant curtain of honeysuckle and clematis. Usually Betsy was one of that group, and very often Peter was, too.

At first Mrs. Marshall would bring Peter in the family car, and then go on to spend an hour or two with some of her friends before returning to pick him up. After a while, Peter began to walk to and from the old Cunningham place. Betsy's heart always ached as she saw him come along the weed-grown drive, the tip of his stick cautiously feeling its way ahead of him, as though it led him.

The first time she saw him come up the drive, she couldn't restrain herself from springing to her feet and running to meet him, guiding him to the steps. But the feel of his arm, rigid with protest against the hand she slipped through it, struck at her like a blow. And she knew that once again she had hurt and hindered him, when she had wanted so passionately to help. She had stood back, dismayed, as Peter walked up the steps past her to seat himself beside Marcia in the old canvas swing. After that, she made herself sit still, her hands clenched tightly in her lap. She wouldn't help him; she wouldn't spring to his aid, she told herself, not even if he stumbled and fell. She wouldn't – because he didn't want her to!

But the knowledge that Peter did not want her help, any more than he wanted her love, was a blinding pain in her.

She talked it all out to Professor Hartley, because he alone, of all the people she knew, understood. He listened, and his old face was touched with pity, but he knew that he could do nothing for her.

"It isn't so much that he resents your trying to guide him, Betsy," he told her one afternoon, as they sat in his garden. "It's that – well, a blind man learns to walk, to find his way about, by counting the steps. When Peter sets out from his place to the Cunningham house, he knows exactly how many steps it takes to reach the drive; how many steps from the street to the porch; how many steps to climb to the porch and to reach his favorite chair."

"Which, of course, is always the swing where Marcia holds court," said Betsy.

Professor Hartley turned his sightless eyes toward her, but she was too absorbed in her own unhappy thoughts to realize that he was suddenly tense.

"He goes instinctively to sit beside Mrs. Eldon?" he asked, after a moment.

"Sure. Oh, she understands him, I guess, and that makes him grateful." Betsy tried hard to make her meaning clear. "She's a pretty swell person. Of course she's not in love with him, and I don't suppose she'd care a lot if he stumbled or fell!"

Professor Hartley was silent for a while, and then he said, "Could you bring Peter to see me, Betsy? I'd like very much to see what he's like."

"I could bring him, of course. He'd be glad to come. He wants to thank you for Gus. He's been wanting to come, but up until the night Marcia gave that dinner party, he's been sort of shy about meeting people."

"He's fond of Gus?" asked the professor.

"Oh, sure. He's crazy about Gus. But he won't let Gus help him. He won't let *anybody* help him," Betsy burst out. "He says Gus is much too good a dog to spend his life hauling some 'big lug' around. That's the way he expressed it."

The professor nodded. "Well, suppose you bring him out, Betsy, any time at all. I'm always at home. He sounds quite a person."

So Betsy took Peter to see Professor Hartley. As always the two little words – "to see" – hurt her. As she and Peter walked across the lawn to where the old man sat beneath his favorite oak, Gus bounded ahead, overcome with delight at being back in a familiar, loved place. Tamar came to meet him, and the two dogs scampered off together.

The professor shook hands with Peter and the two men, both sightless, faced each other, as if by some miracle they could see with a clarity forbidden to physical eyes.

"It's good to see you, Peter," said the older man.

"Thank you, sir. It's good to see you," said Peter. "I've wanted to thank you for Gus."

"Don't thank me, Peter. Gus is Betsy's gift to you. She trained him herself. I hope he is justifying that training by being very helpful to you?"

Peter's jaw tightened a little. "Oh, I manage to get about without using Gus as a guide. Thanks to the fellows at the Rehabilitation Center, I learned to get along

73

very well. If only people would let me alone! I know exactly where I'm going and how many steps it takes to get there – if only somebody doesn't make me lose count. Then I'm really lost."

Betsy paled a little, but knew that if she kept still they would not be aware of her tension. When she was sure she could manage her voice she said:

"May I make tea, Professor – or coffee?"

The old man turned to her, smiling. "That would be very nice, my dear," he said, sensing her need for escape. "But you must promise to put everything back exactly in its own spot when you've finished."

"I learned that a long time ago," Betsy told him, and fled.

As she went she heard him saying to Peter, "Every piece of furniture in my house is fastened to the floor. And everything in the kitchen has its own spot and must be put back there when not in use. It's the only way I can be sure of getting around, or of cooking the thing I happen to want to cook."

When the screen door had banged shut behind Betsy, he said, "She's a wonderful little person, isn't she?"

"Betsy? Oh, Betsy's a swell kid – a little like an over-enthusiastic puppy that insists on climbing up your trousers, even if his paws are muddy!" Peter spoke lightly, and his companion could catch no undertone in his voice to indicate that he meant more or less than what he was saying.

"But now that she's not a kid any more, now that she's quite grown up – "

"Oh, Betsy's not grown up. Far from it!" protested Peter. "Well, of course, I suppose she *has* grown up to a certain extent; but I'm afraid she'll always be an infant to me – the way she was when I saw her last."

"Yes, of course. That's inevitable."

For a moment the two men were silent. Before them the lawn was a velvety green; the sunlight, which lay over it in a golden wash, was broken here and there by the shadows beneath the ancient trees. In the perennial garden, bees hummed drowsily. The afternoon was too hot, for bird-song, though an occasional sparrow, startled perhaps by some prowling cat, made short, sharp sounds of anger.

Both men sensed the loveliness that they could not see: the warmth of the sun; the cool, faint breeze that stirred the trees to mysterious murmurings; the protesting birds; the bees' drowsy humming. All were sights locked tightly in their memories, to be sounds from now on; sights that would never grow less beautiful, less poignant with the march of the years; memories that would deepen and grow more beautiful.

The older man stirred and cleared his throat. He turned his sightless eyes upon Peter and asked curiously:

"What had you planned to come home to, Peter, if things had gone differently?"

Peter's jaw hardened, and there was, for a moment, a taut, white line about his mouth.

"Oh, the usual thing, I suppose. A job I liked; perhaps a wife and children. What does any fellow my age plan?"

"What sort of job?" probed the professor, careful that there could be no hint of idle curiosity in his voice.

Peter gave a short, little laugh. "I was studying to be an architect. One of the few things no man denied his eyesight could ever hope to be."

"That's too bad. But at least you can fulfill the rest of your dream."

Peter's head jerked around. "You mean I can still hope to marry, have children? Good Lord, man, are you insane?" he snapped. "Do you think I'd saddle any woman with the burden of a helpless husband?"

"You're not helpless, Peter, unless you want it that way."

76

Peter was on his feet now. His host sensed the swift, angry movement.

"Helpless to give any normal woman the kind of life she's entitled to," Peter said shortly. "No, thanks, Professor Hartley. I couldn't do that to any woman."

"But if she loved you?"

"If she loved me, that would be all the more reason why I couldn't," said Peter through his teeth.

"You're taking a very narrow view, my boy."

"Sorry, sir. I can't agree with you."

There was a taut silence, the slight creak of the wicker chair as Peter sat down again. The older man searched his mind for something he could say that might help the boy beside him. He knew how desperately Peter needed the help he was too proud and too stubborn – and too young – to ask for. When he spoke at last, it was on a subject far removed from what they had been discussing.

"I suppose things were pretty bad out there in Vietnam," he said quietly.

"Well, it wasn't exactly a picnic," returned Peter.

"No, I imagine not. I suppose, if a handful of you Yanks had been suddenly faced with an overwhelming number of the enemy, you'd have fought it out to the last man, rather than surrender?"

"Good grief, *yes!*" Peter all but exploded.

"Yet when you come home, and the odds seem overwhelmingly against you?" suggested the older man, but he did not finish the sentence.

"I'm afraid I don't quite get you, sir." Peter's voice was a little strained, as though with the effort to control his temper.

"I suppose I am – well, I suppose I sound offensive." Professor Hartley spoke with a disarming gentleness that robbed his words of any possible sting. "It's just that I've travelled a long, long way down the road you've just begun, my boy. It's probably presumptuous of me to offer you any counsel, yet I'd feel I had failed you – and Betsy, as well – if I didn't."

"What's Betsy got to do with my problems?" Peter cut in.

"Nothing, I suppose, except that she is very fond of you and deeply concerned about your happiness. Since it was through Betsy that I first knew anything about you, I suppose it's quite natural that I should associate you together. What I meant to say was that it's a long, dark, lonely road, my boy. Yet if you face it with courage and strength, it need not be lonely. Love is – well, love is like a light that can open up even the darkness in which you and I are destined to travel."

"No, thanks."

The old man sighed.

"How well I know how you feel – and how it brings back my own past," he said after a moment. "Of course, my position was different in many ways. I was poor. I had been blinded in a chemical experiment in the school laboratory, so there was none of the glory that surrounds a war hero."

Peter's lips twisted derisively. "We'll skip the war hero stuff, if you don't mind, sir."

"Of course. I know you would feel that way. I had no such feeling. I mean, there was no excuse for me to feel that I had been anything but inexcusably careless, and deeply grateful that I had been alone when I was making the experiment, so that I, alone, suffered the consequences," the older man went on, and now there was a faintly bitter twist to his mouth. "I learned too late that when fooling with dangerous chemicals, one must keep one's mind on the chemicals, and not go moon-gazing after even the most beautiful of women. But it was spring, and I was reasonably certain that she was not entirely indifferent to me."

"You were in love?" asked Peter, momentarily forgetting his own bitterness. Then he added, "Afterwards, of course, she threw you over. That's usually the case."

"She did nothing of the kind," the old man said sharply. "She came to me, putting aside her pride and her dignity, and begged me to marry her. But I was too stiff-necked. I had too much pride to be a burden even to the woman who loved me, as I loved her. You see, I was so sure that my helplessness *would* be a burden to her; I hadn't learned yet that love asks, more than anything else, to be needed – and used. Love wants to serve."

He heard Peter's little movement of protest, and waited tensely for his voice. But Peter made no comment.

"Of course," Professor Hartley went on, after a moment, "I suppose if I'd had enough money to support us both, I'd have gone through with it. But I knew she'd have to work to earn enough for us to live on. And to see her saddled with a husband who would be more helpless than a baby – well, I just couldn't take it. I hadn't learned, you see, that being blind doesn't necessarily mean being helpless."

He paused, as if waiting for Peter to speak,

but the young man still remained silent, so he continued:

"For the first five years of my blindness I played the part of a coward. I even tried to destroy myself. All that helped me to keep sane was a friend. He took care of me, shared his small earnings with me. And when he died, I found he had left me this cottage with two acres of land and a little annuity. It was the death of my friend that proved to me that my disability was a challenge, and that I had to face up to it. After a friend had sacrificed so much to me – "

"But at least you hadn't sacrificed the woman you loved," said Peter.

"No, but it wasn't until years later that I realized it wouldn't have been a sacrifice," said the old man. "It wouldn't be a sacrifice for the woman who loves you, Peter. At least there would not be the economic problem. You could still have a rich, full life, children – "

"No, thanks!"

The professor made a little gesture of futility. "Forgive me, Peter," he said. "I know I've seemed presumptuous. Forgive an old man's concern."

"Sure. It's all right, sir, thanks," said Peter hurriedly, because he had heard the sound of Betsy's footsteps on the flagged path.

She was carrying a laden tray. There were three tall glasses of iced tea, tangy with fresh mint, and a platter of little cakes. As she put the tray down on the table, she looked anxiously from one to the other, and said:

"All right, gentlemen, your favorite tipple! And some cakes I swiped from Esther this morning. Mother's having a bridge-fight this afternoon, and Esther made some grand-looking stuff, I thought we might as well have some of the party!"

With her coming, the tension left the two men. Betsy was gay and amusing, and they followed her every movement with sightless eyes. But when she saw a warm, friendly grin on Peter's face she had hard work not to burst into happy tears.

When at last they rose to go, and Betsy whistled to Gus, Peter said to their host, "Thanks for everything, sir. I'd like to come again, if I may."

"I hope you will, my boy, as often as you can endure the company of an old man! You will be more than welcome."

As he followed Betsy to the car and felt his way to the seat, Peter said, "You've got some nice friends, chick. The professor's tops."

"He's a darling," said Betsy simply. "I adore him."

"And he loves you," said Peter.

82

There were little flags of color in her cheeks, but she managed to say in a casual voice, "Sure. Love begets love. Didn't you know that? He'd have to love me, because I love him. It always works out like that – or didn't you know?"

She all but held her breath for his answer. She fixed her eyes on his face, causing the car to wobble a little as she failed to give it proper attention. But Peter was thinking, and for the moment unconscious of the car's swerve.

"'Love begets, love' eh?" he repeated. "Where'd you read that, Betsy?"

Betsy caught the note of tension in his voice, and her heart did a crazy little upward surge. "Oh, I don't know. Somewhere. Anyway, it's a universal fact, recognized by – oh, by people like Freud, and such," she answered him with unconvincing airiness.

Peter was sitting with his sightless eyes turned straight ahead, his hands, clenched on the top of his cane.

"So?" he said at last. "You mean if you love someone very deeply, with all your heart, that someone will, given time, learn to love you?"

Betsy's eyes were shining. But above the tumult in her heart she said with forced gaiety:

"But of course. Any dope knows *that!*"

Peter turned his head, as though looking down at her, and suddenly he grinned. "You're very convincing, pet," he told her. "But it seems to me I've heard differently."

Betsy laughed, shakily. "Oh, well, you believe what you believe, and I'll believe what I believe, and we can still be friends – being the broad-minded type!" she answered.

Peter laughed, and when Betsy let him out at his house a little later, she could tell by the way he smiled that he was happier than he had been when they set out.

Chapter Eight

That evening after dinner, when George had left for his weekly lodge meeting, Edith and Betsy were alone in the living room. There was a far-away look in Betsy's eyes, and Edith waited for some clue to her daughter's secret thoughts. But when Betsy was ready to confide, she would – and not a moment before.

"Mum," she said presently, and Edith's heart warmed at the old childhood term, "do you think it's true that if you love somebody – well, pretty terribly – that somebody sort of *has* to love you in return?"

Edith's eyes widened and then she dropped them to her sewing.

"Well, in a way, I suppose it's true," she admitted. "It's natural enough. If you love a person, you naturally show him your best and most attractive self. You work at the job of winning his love. And I suppose if you work at anything long enough and hard enough, you get what you're after."

Betsy was watching her, listening intently, and there was something in her golden-brown eyes that stabbed at her mother's heart.

"It's Peter, I suppose?" Edith asked, impulsively.

Betsy's eyebrows went up a little and she seemed to retreat. But she answered promptly, "Of course. Who else? It's always been Pete and it always will be!"

"But darling, Pete's *blind*. Surely, you must realize – " Edith stopped, halted by the look on her daughter's face.

"And that only makes me love him all the more. Because I can help him and take care of him – and do things for him," Betsy said quietly.

"I know, darling – but Pete's not in love with you." Edith's voice shook a little.

"I know that, Mother." Betsy's face seemed drained of all color. "He's not in love with me *now*. But if I work very hard, and do everything I can to make him realize I'm all grown up and everything – "

Edith waited, not daring to speak, lest she say the wrong thing. This business of being a parent was complicated, she told herself. It was hard to stand aside and watch the daughter you adored rush headlong into a furnace. But if the child wouldn't let you help . . .

"Do you suppose if I let somebody give

me a terrific rush and get myself engaged, that would make Pete realize I'm grown up?" suggested Betsy. "I mean, if I were engaged to somebody else, then he'd know I'm old enough to be married."

"Betsy Drummond! Are you out of your mind?" raged Edith. "Of all the shameless – "

"Bo Norris wouldn't mind being engaged to me," Betsy said coolly.

"Any man would mind being used in such a shameless, cruel way." Edith was appalled at the revelation of Betsy's deviousness. "Why, poor Bo has been mad about you for years. He'd all but lose his mind if he thought you'd give him a kind word, let alone promise to marry him."

"Then why shouldn't I let him have a little fun? At least, if Pete thought I was going to marry Bo, he might decide he didn't want to lose me himself."

Edith was aghast. "Betsy, I honestly believe you mean that," she whispered.

Betsy's head went up. "There's very little I wouldn't do to get Pete," she acknowledged.

Edith drew a deep breath and pricked herself with her forgotten needle, and realized that she was shaking. "Well, this is one thing you're not going to do, Betsy. I won't permit it!"

Betsy said nothing, but with eyes cool and almost inimical, she gave her mother a look that said more plainly than words, "Oh. And how are you going to stop me?"

"You just make one play for poor Bo and, so help me, I'll tell him the truth."

Betsy regarded her for a moment, and then she said coolly, "Okay, then. I guess that's out. I'll have to think of something else."

She went back to her book as calmly as though nothing had happened. Edith, trying to go back to her sewing, found her eyes blurred by tears and her hands shaking so that she dared not continue.

She was appalled at the revelation Betsy had made – Betsy, her beloved child, on whose kindliness and generosity she had always banked. Here was Betsy callously proposing to get herself engaged to one man simply to convince another man that she was old enough for marriage! Suddenly Edith had the unhappy conviction that this girl who sat across from her was a stranger – and a stranger of whom she was a little frightened. She was secretly glad when, a little later, Betsy yawned and said good night.

Edith sat on alone, until she heard the door

close at the top of the stairs. Then she put her face in her hands and burst into tears.

She was startled when she heard George's footsteps and looked up at the clock to see that it was eleven-thirty. George came in, looking pleased and relaxed.

Chapter Nine

Several days after Betsy's suggestion that she become engaged to Bo Norris, Edith, Molly Prior and Anne Hutchens were sitting in Edith's garden. It was a pleasant place, with the shade of the friendly old trees, and with the white-painted garden furniture.

"How about calling Marcia and having a game?" suggested Molly.

"Maybe she's getting too young in her ideas to want to play about with us," said Anne, her eyes malicious.

"I'm not so sure I like that," Molly said frankly.

"Just what part of my innocent remark upsets you most, darling?" cooed Anne.

"None of it, pet," answered Molly. "I meant that I'm not too crazy about our kids gathering at the feet of Marcia Eldon. Bobbie's been going around mooning lately, and I've got my fingers crossed. For a while I was sure he was going to marry Anne Gray, and I was glad. She's exactly the sort of girl I'd select for a daughter-in-law. But all of a sudden, Bobbie stopped seeing her, and he hangs around Marcia Eldon until I could scream."

"I'd say she is pretty potent stuff for unsophisticated kids like yours," announced Anne. "But the thing that throws me is that Peter Marshall seems to be practically living there these days."

"Anne!" Edith cried sharply.

"What have I said *now?* " asked Anne.

Molly answered. "Since you've become a lady-in-waiting, darling, your tongue has grown much too sharp, don't you think?"

Anne pulled herself almost erect in the long garden chair, and her blue eyes were wide, her expression much too innocent to be convincing.

"Don't be absurd, Molly! All I said was that Peter is at Marcia Eldon's from dawn until midnight. It's quite true, and I don't see why anybody should get excited about it! After all, Peter's free and twenty-one; and Marcia is free – supposedly – and more than twenty-one. So what if they do see a lot of each other?"

Molly eyed her sternly. "What do you mean – Marcia's *supposedly* free?" she demanded.

Anne shrugged. "Oh, all I know is that we were playing bridge at Stacy Allen's house last week – Marcia and I were partners. And while Jennie Stewart was dealing, she asked, with that poison sweetness of hers, 'Will Mr. Eldon be joining you here this summer, Mrs. Eldon?' Of course there was a silence in which you could have heard a pin-feather drop. But Marcia only smiled and said, 'I sincerely hope not. I'm afraid his wife wouldn't approve. She's rather narrow-minded about such things as ex-wives, you see."

"Divorced!" breathed Molly.

"Obviously," answered Anne.

Edith made no comment, and after a moment Anne stirred a little and said pettishly, "Oh, well, I thought it was rather exciting news, after all. We've been wondering about her, and why she is a Mrs. without a Mr. around, and now we know."

"Yes," said Molly. "And now I'm really worried about Bobbie!"

"You needn't be," said Anne. "Bobbie's got a head on his shoulders, and he's been around. He'll see through her, in time."

"But suppose there's nothing to see," said Edith quietly. "After all, we're a bunch of spiteful, malicious cats. Just because Marcia is a stranger here, and people are beginning to make a fuss over her, could it be that we are jealous?"

"If by 'people' you mean all the

unattached young men about town – and a few of the older unattached men, like Mr. Pirkle, whose wife died three years ago, and old Mr. Hewett who has never had a wife – then I'm willing to admit 'people' are making a fuss over her," said Molly flatly. "But I haven't heard the girls or our own friends raving about her."

"Betsy is devoted to her," announced Edith.

There was a moment of tension, but almost before they had time to be conscious of it, it was gone.

"Oh, well, Betsy's a sweetheart, and she's as friendly as a puppy," said Molly. "And anyway, Marcia's not making a play for Betsy's young man –"

"But I always thought Betsy was mad about Peter Marshall," Anne broke in.

Molly gave her a warning glance, but her voice was elaborately casual as she said, "Now you're talking nonsense, Anne. You know very well that Betsy and Pete have been pals for years. Betsy's not in love with anybody."

"No?" asked Anne, sweetly.

"No!" returned Molly. "Betsy's not even grown up."

"Betsy's nineteen," Anne pointed out.

"How did my child get mixed up in this?"

Edith put a determinedly good-natured end to the argument. "As I remember it, we suggested that we ask Marcia to come over and make up a table of bridge. How we got tangled up in all this gossip, I'm sure I don't know. Hold everything while I telephone her."

She went across the grass, and Molly turned to Anne and said in a savage undertone, "Anne Hutchens, if you want that baby of yours to be born before I murder you with my bare hands, you'll keep that little trap of yours shut about Peter Marshall and Betsy."

Anne regarded her coolly. "I think Betsy ought to know that Pete is at Marcia Eldon's place every day, and practically *all* day," she said. "You and I both know Betsy worships Pete. And I can't imagine what Marcia means. After all, she is almost twice as old as he is."

"Whoa there!" ordered Molly. "Peter's about twenty-four, and Marcia Eldon can't be more than twenty-eight."

"Ever see her in the good strong sunlight? She'll never see thirty-five again."

"Don't be an idiot. She's only two or three years older than Peter, and marriage between people their ages is by no means unusual," Molly pointed out, without realizing what

94

she was saying. The next moment, her eyes widened and she looked startled.

Anne, watching her, chuckled. "See what I mean?" she drawled.

"But – oh, for Heaven's sake, Anne –"

"Molly, you're so blind," observed Anne. "We all know Marcia Eldon hasn't a cent. She deposits fifty dollars in the bank on the first of every month, and before the end of the month she's having to dip into that reserve fund she opened her account with. Never mind how I know – I *know!* The five hundred is almost gone, and the fifty dollars goes nowhere at all."

"So what?" demanded Molly.

"So the Marshalls are wealthy. Old Mr. Marshall, Pete's father, left a two hundred and fifty thousand dollar trust fund for Peter, and Mrs. Marshall is adequately provided for. I'd say that Marcia Eldon would be mighty glad to get her hands on the Marshall money – wouldn't you? And Pete, even if he is blind, is not unattractive. He's really sweet. Gilded with two hundred and fifty thousand, I'd say he would be pretty easy to take."

For the moment Molly couldn't think of anything to say. Secretly she was relieved at the thought that Marcia couldn't possibly have any designs on Bobbie, because the Priors were not wealthy and Bobbie was dependent on his modest salary for a living. It would be two or three years before he could think of getting married. . . .

Meanwhile, Edith had picked up the telephone and given the number of the house next door, across the lawn and through the unclipped hedge. She waited, and then a man's voice said, "Hello?"

It was Peter's voice, and Edith recognized it instantly. She felt a vague sinking of her heart, but she answered him promptly.

"Hello, Peter. Is Mrs. Eldon there? This is Edith Drummond."

"Oh, how are you, Mrs. Drummond? Just a minute and I'll call Marcia."

She heard Peter go away from the telephone, and, after a moment, footsteps coming closer, then a burst of smothered laughter.

"Hello, Mrs. Drummond." Marcia's voice was light with laughter – laughter accompanied by Peter's over some trivial incident, perhaps, that had been amusing only because they had shared it.

"I didn't know you had company, Mrs. Eldon," said Edith, and could not keep her voice from sounding formal. "Mrs. Prior and Mrs. Hutchens are here, and we thought you might like to take a hand at bridge."

"That was sweet of you to think of me,

Mrs. Drummond," said Marcia politely. "But I'm afraid I shall have to ask you to give me a rain-check. There are some people here."

"Yes, of course – some other time, then."

After she had put the telephone down, Edith stood for a moment, just staring at it, thinking. Peter had seemed so completely at home. He had answered the telephone; he had shared laughter with Marcia, and the telephone had given no indication of other voices. Yet Marcia had said, "Some people are here." Edith knew instinctively that there was no one there but Peter, and tried to deny the little stab of pain at her heart. Pain for Betsy, who might be terribly hurt. Betsy was so completely in love with Peter.

She tried to laugh at herself, to scold herself. She had not been happy about Betsy's love for Peter; from the first, knowing Peter, she had not believed that he returned her love, and Betsy would inevitably be hurt. But now that Peter was obviously in love with Marcia . . .

She made herself go back to the two women who were waiting in the garden, carrying three bottles of Coca-cola and three glasses and a plate of cookies on a tray, as an excuse for her long absence.

"Is she coming over?" asked Anne, reaching for a cookie.

"No, she's got guests," answered Edith.

"Oh," said Anne, regarding the depths of her glass with elaborate interest. "So she has guests? Am I surprised! And of course, Peter Marshall is one of them."

"I believe so," said Edith curtly.

Molly glanced at Anne, but refrained from making any comment.

The rest of the afternoon moved with a jerkiness that was completely foreign to the three friends, and Edith was secretly relieved when Anne decided it was time to leave. She walked with them to the gate, and stood there in the warm sunlight, watching them until Molly's car turned from sight.

She didn't know quite how long she stood there, but at last she heard footsteps coming toward her, and looked up. A tall young man in slacks and a shirt with an open collar, the sleeves turned back to his elbows, came toward her. Beside him paced a beautiful dog. It was, of course, Peter Marshall and the dog, Gus.

"Hello, Peter." Edith made her voice sound warm and friendly, and was ashamed that she did not feel like that toward Peter at the moment.

"Oh, hello, Mrs. Drummond," said Peter, and paused.

"Your dog's a beauty, Peter," said Edith, embarrassed because she could think of nothing less inane to say.

"Oh, Gus is quite a pooch," answered Peter. "Betsy was a sweetheart to get him for me. I'm afraid she's a little annoyed with me, though, that I don't let him drag me about at the end of a wooden harness!"

"I suppose Betsy feels that Gus would be happier if you made use of his training." Edith was uncomfortably aware that there was a faint edge to her voice.

She saw the taut line about Peter's mouth, as he said curtly, "It's not much of a life for a pup, hauling a guy around. I like it better this way, and I'm sure Gus does, too."

"Well, of course that's something for you to decide."

A car slithered to the curb with a screaming of tortured brakes, and Betsy called out eagerly, "Hello, Pete? Want a lift? I'm going your way."

"Hi, scrap. Sure it won't take you out of your way?" said Peter. He turned his face toward Betsy, and Edith could have wept at the radiant look in the girl's eyes. It was a look that laid Betsy's young heart bare for anyone to see its small secret, which was, in reality, a secret to no one but Peter.

"How could it be?" Betsy was saying now. "I just said I was going your way. Hello Gus – want to ride? He's a sucker for a car," she added proudly, as Gus, leaning lightly against Peter's knees, steered him toward the car.

"Well, stop shoving, darn you!" Peter ordered the dog. "I'm coming."

But Gus would not get into the car until Peter was settled. Then he leaped in agilely and sat up on his haunches, his pink tongue lolling in delight.

"Don't be late for supper, Betsy. I'm making strawberry shortcake," said Edith.

Betsy turned to Peter. "Stay for supper, Pete?" she begged. "Mom makes the best shortcake in the world!"

Peter laughed. "Thanks, I'd like to, only I promised Mother I'd be home for supper. There's a rumor going the rounds that she's making shortcake, too. She'd put arsenic in my soup if I failed to show up."

"Some other time, then, eh, Pete?" said Betsy, and Edith wasn't quite sure whether she wanted to cry, or to shake Betsy for being so transparent.

"Any time, Peter. We're always glad to

100

have you," Edith echoed her daughter's hospitality.

"Thanks, that's swell of you," said Pete.

Betsy put the little car in motion, and Edith went back to the house, her heart heavy within her. To see so clearly the heartbreak toward which Betsy was rushing, and not to be able to lay so much as a feather in her path to check that flight, seemed almost more than she could endure.

Chapter Ten

Bowling along the road that brief mile to Peter's home, Betsy wished she could think of some way to prolong the drive. "And yet," she reflected unhappily, "even if I could think of a way, I wouldn't dare try it. Pete would only insist on going straight home, and that would be too – too humiliating." So she put the thought aside, and said, chattily:

"Marcia's a grand person, isn't she?"

"Wonderful." The tone of Peter's voice made the word a paean of praise. In fact, it was said with such simple conviction, such sincerity, that Betsy blinked a little.

"Look here, pal, you aren't getting crazy ideas about Marcia, are you?" she demanded.

Pete's smile faded. "I'm afraid I don't quite get you," he said.

"Oh, I mean you aren't doing anything so ridiculous as imagining you're in love with Marcia – gosh, that's a laugh, isn't it. Where in the world do you suppose I ever got such an idea?" she chattered inanely, but her eyes were dark with apprehension.

"Can't a man admire a grand girl like Marcia without falling in love with her?"

"I don't know," said Betsy, her voice shaking a little. "You tell me!"

Peter's taut young face, the thin-lipped mouth bracketed by two white lines, was turned straight ahead and Betsy saw his hands gripped stoutly about his cane.

"Wouldn't I be a pretty fool to allow myself to fall in love with *any* woman – let alone one as beautiful and desirable as Marcia Eldon?" Peter's voice was thick with bitterness.

Betsy was silent for a moment. When she spoke, she tried hard to sound flippant, but didn't succeed. She only sounded frightened and hurt.

"*Allow?* Who ever heard of anybody allowing himself to fall in love, Peter?" she demanded. "I don't believe anybody really *wants* to fall in love. It's just one of those things. You go along all peaceful and happy and minding your own business – and then *wham!* There you are – head over heels in misery! And there isn't one single thing you can do about it!"

Peter was facing her now, as though staring at her behind the dark glasses.

"The Voice of Experience," he chided her, and tried to match her attempt at flippancy.

"You certainly make being in love sound like a wonderful experience."

"Being in love is ghastly, and I hate it. I wish I could stop. That's the plain, unadulterated, concentrated devilishness of it – you can't stop!"

Peter looked startled and sorry. "Betsy, child, you're all wrong," he protested. "Being in love is – well, it's a glorious experience!"

"It's nothing of the kind!" exclaimed Betsy. "Oh, I know people write gushy songs about the glories of being in love, and they write books and make movies about it. But take it from me, pal, it's the bunk! That is, of course, unless you have the colossal luck to fall in love with somebody who loves you. Even then I don't think it would be all gravy."

She paused a moment, then went on, breathlessly:

"You never know an easy moment. You're worried, if you're with him, for fear you'll do something he won't like. And if you're not with him, you're wondering where he is and afraid maybe he's finding somebody he likes better than you. You spend hours hovering around your telephone, praying for it to ring. And when it does, nine times out of ten, it's the wrong number. And then, when you *do*

104

get to be with him, you're all tongue-tied. You can't make bright conversation, and you decide that he's convinced you're a dope."

"Hey, Bets – hold it up! Where did you ever garner so much profound wisdom? Or is it just crazy talk? You're too young to know so much!" protested Peter, frowning.

Betsy looked at him. She could look at him all she liked and she didn't have to be careful of her expression, of the revelation of her eyes, because Pete, poor darling, couldn't see her. She blinked back the tears and brought the car to a halt in the driveway of the Marshall home.

"I've had years of experience," she told Peter after a moment, "I've been in love since I was twelve!"

Peter looked slightly annoyed. "Betsy, Betsy – you're still playing with dolls!" he scolded. "You're still just a kid. You don't know the first thing about love."

"Bo Norris thinks I'm grown up enough to marry him, and maybe I will!" she announced with a calmness that surprised her.

But the look that flashed across Peter's face was the most cruel blow she had ever received. It was one of acute relief! Peter was *glad* she was going to marry Bo! She had thought the news would shake him into a realization that he himself was in love with her – and, instead, he had looked relieved!

"Bo Norris, eh?" he was saying now. "Well, that's great, Betsy. Bo's a grand guy! Congratulations. I'll send you a set of solid silver pickleforks for your wedding present."

"And I'll take good care of them, and send them back to you when you and Marcia get married," Betsy said through her teeth.

Instantly the laughter faded from Peter's face, and it was stern again. His hands tightened on the cane, and his body went rigid.

"I'm afraid you'll keep 'em for life, then, Betsy. For the Lord's sake, do you suppose I'd ask any woman to share the sort of life I lead?" he burst out savagely.

"She'd like it – if she loved you."

"But Marcia's not in love with me."

"No, I suppose not," Betsy agreed with perfect sincerity. "But she'll marry you like a flash if you want her to."

Peter was still for a moment, but his expression told her it was only to control his temper. Then he said bitingly, "Marcia has never struck me as the sort of woman to make such a sacrifice for a 'wounded hero.'" The last two words came with such bitterness that Betsy shrank a little.

"Well, gosh, who ever said it would be a

sacrifice to marry you, Pete, you idiot?" she demanded. "Anyway, Marcia would marry you like a shot. She's tired of being poor."

"That's enough!" snapped Peter.

"Well, don't snap my head off," Betsy protested, with some heat: "Marcia's ambitious. She's – well, she's glamorous and all that, but she's practical, too. She hasn't any money, and she needs a lot of it to go on studying to be a great singer."

"And you're suggesting that she would tie herself to a useless hulk like me, just because my ancestors happened to be thrifty and were kind enough to leave me money? Well, thanks a lot, Betsy. I thought you were a friend of Marcia's. I never suspected you of being a malicious spiteful little cat!"

"I'm not! I'm not a cat! I like Marcia. But that doesn't mean I'm too stupid to understand her," Betsy raged. "I know how ambitious she is. I've heard her say, 'Nothing is ever going to stand in my way again. I'm a singer, I'm going to be a great singer, and nothing's going to stop me."

"And is being ambitious a disgrace?"

"No, and marrying a man you don't love, if he will help you to realize your ambition isn't a disgrace, either, I suppose?"

Suddenly Peter laughed. It wasn't a very pleasant laugh, and his face looked tired.

"Betsy, my sweet," he said dryly, "we're a couple of fools. Here we sit arguing and throwing brick-bats at each other, and all because of a woman who would laugh her head off if she so much as suspected I'm in love with her."

"Then you *are* in love with her."

Peter nodded. "Now go ahead and laugh."

Betsy was still for what seemed like a long, long time. It might have been a matter of moments; it was probably no more than seconds, but it was long enough for her to watch the dearest dream of her life shrivel and die.

"I'm laughing fit to kill," she said at last, in a voice so low that Peter could scarcely distinguish the words.

"You should be, Betsy. It's very amusing," he said bitterly. "I thought the day they told me I was hopelessly blind was the worst day of my life. I know now it was only a sort of curtain raiser. To be hopelessly in love is far worse than to be hopelessly blind."

Betsy sat very still. Even in this devastating moment of her own life, her first instinct was to help him, to offer comfort. It was a mark of the measure of her love that his happiness seemed more important than hers.

"It needn't be a tragedy, Pete, unless you want it to," she told him. "She will marry you. She'd like to! I've seen the way she looks at you."

Peter turned to her sharply, but before the expression of hope could more than flicker across his face, it was gone. "Don't, Betsy. Don't build me up with false hopes. If I thought for a moment that she cared for me –"

With her usual devastating honesty, Betsy blurted out, "Oh, don't get me wrong. I don't think Marcia's in love with you. I don't think she's in love with anybody. I don't believe she's capable of loving anybody but herself. I only said she'd marry you, if you wanted her to."

Peter's eyebrows went up a little. "Charming picture, Betsy. You make Marcia sound enchanting." He fumbled for the catch of the car door, and swung it open.

Gus, alert since the moment the car had stopped, was already on the sidewalk. As Peter climbed out of the car, Gus pressed against him, and Peter, in a moment of rare annoyance with the dog, said sharply, "Hang it, stop shoving me!"

"Stop shouting at him!" Betsy blazed. "If you'd give him a chance to do the thing he's been trained to do –"

"I will *not* be hauled around at the end of a wooden harness by a dog that deserves a better break!"

"Gus has been trained to be of service to the one he loves – and that happens to be you! If you weren't so pig-headed and stubborn, you'd have sense enough to know that love likes to serve."

With that parting shot, Betsy sent the car racing off down the street, so blinded by tears that she could scarcely see how to drive.

"Betsy!" Pete called out. "Wait a minute!"

He had taken a hasty step toward the sound of the car. That unconsidered step took him off the sidewalk, and he stumbled, just as another car came down the street. With lightning-like speed, Gus leaped forward, sending Pete sprawling, but out of the way of the car.

Peter put his hand down, and Gus lifted his head to meet it. Peter fondled the big, satiny head, the velvety pointed ears, and felt the powerful neck that he had sworn never to harness; and suddenly he was acutely ashamed. He had failed Gus.

"Sorry, old man," he said huskily, and if the dog did not understand the words, he caught the note of affection in Peter's voice, and quivered with pleasure. "You win," said Peter. "No, that's not quite right. You lose,

110

old boy. But maybe that's the way you'd like it. Betsy said love wants to serve. Well, you shall serve, Gus. I'll try to make it up to you, some way. You're still going to have freedom and fun, but I guess from here on out, the two of us will walk in step, huh?"

Chapter Eleven

It was late afternoon when Professor Hartley heard Betsy coming across the lawn. It was almost as though his thoughts had evoked her physical presence, and he turned his face toward the sound of her steps, making himself smile warmly.

"Hello, Betsy, my dear. Come and sit down! I'm so glad to see you," he said.

Betsy eyed him with suspicion. "What's wrong? You're not holding out on me? You haven't been ill, or upset or anything, and trying not to let me know?"

"Of course not, child." He urged her to the chair near him. "I guess it's the heat. I'm a little tired."

"Been hoeing the garden?" she demanded sternly. "I warned you not to, or to weed the flower beds. I told you I'd do it."

"I haven't been doing anything, my dear, but sitting here like a lazy old cat basking in the sunlight," he assured her.

Betsy dropped into the chair, accepting his statement, and plunging instantly into the reason for her coming.

112

"I wanted to tell you, Professor Hartley, that Pete is letting Gus help him. Isn't that wonderful? I saw them a little while ago. Gus had his harness on, and he was laughing fit to kill, and he looked so proud of himself. He's been so confused and unhappy because Peter wouldn't let him work – isn't that marvelous?" she chattered.

"Yes, I know. Peter was out here this morning."

"Oh, what for?"

The professor tried to laugh. "Must my friends always have a reason for coming to see me?"

"Well, I always have one," Betsy told him. "I come to see you because I love you."

"That's very sweet of you, Betsy – thank you."

"And now, why did Peter come this morning?"

The old man hesitated. Yet would it not be kinder if someone she loved and trusted delivered the blow? Wouldn't the merciful brutality of that be kinder than waiting for her to hear it from someone else – perhaps in bits and pieces that would leave her in suspense and anguish?

"He came to ask my advice," said the professor. "He wanted to know if I thought

113

he had the right to ask a woman to marry him."

Betsy was silent. He could not see her; but he sensed her rigidity, the way the color left her face, the young eyes dark with pain.

"Marcia Eldon, of course," she said at last, her voice too faint to have reached ears less keen than those of the man sitting nearby.

"Yes."

Betsy sat very still for a while, and then suddenly her small clenched fists beat at her knees and she said through her teeth, "But she's not good enough for him. She's – spiteful, and malicious, and unkind!"

"Betsy, Betsy, child!"

"I know you think I'm being catty and mean. But truly I'm not. She isn't kind, Professor. I saw her shrink from Peter one day. And the other night when we were having coca-colas, Pete spilled a little. He didn't know it – nobody let on that they noticed it. But Marcia looked at him, and then at Bo Norris and wrinkled her nose in disgust. Bo wanted to smack her. I wish I'd let him – oh, I wish I'd let him!"

The tears had come now, and Betsy was weeping with heartbroken abandon. The professor cleared his throat to steady his voice, and tried to offer consolation.

"But, child, you're behaving as though

he's already engaged to Mrs. Eldon. We don't even know that she'll accept him," he pointed out, without in the least believing it.

"Oh, she'll accept him. She'll marry him so quickly he won't know what happened! And the minute she's finished with him, she'll divorce him. When she gets all she can out of him –" Betsy hid her face behind her shaking hands.

When at last she stood up to go, she said huskily, "Thanks for telling me, Professor Hartley. I'd much rather hear it from you than from anybody else in the world. I know how to protect myself, now. Forewarned is forearmed, isn't it?"

"Betsy, you won't do anything rash? Anything foolish?"

She bent and pressed her tear-wet cheek to his, her arm tight about his shoulders.

"No, Professor – oh, no. I won't do anything foolish! I'm going to be very sensible from here on out!" she told him. "I'll keep you posted."

Then she was gone, running across the lawn and out to the street. A moment later he heard the sound of her little car racing off down the highway.

George and Edith were at dinner when Betsy came in. They had waited for her, and then had decided that she was staying to eat with Professor Hartley. Edith had been a little annoyed that Betsy had been thoughtless enough not to telephone.

They heard her come into the hall, and stand there for a little while, before she came into the dining room and faced them. Her color was high, and her eyes were bright with excitement, but her mouth quivered as she spoke.

"I want you two to be the first to know," she carolled, her voice a little too high, a shade too shrill. "Bo Norris and I are announcing our engagement. It'll be in tomorrow's paper."

"*Betsy!*" Edith gasped.

"Aren't you being a little premature?" demanded George. "Maybe I'm old-fashioned, but I thought a father and mother were at least consulted – or notified –"

"I'm notifying you now, Pops," said Betsy with that unconvincing gaiety. "And there wasn't a lot of time. After all, I can't have the whole town thinking I married Bo just because Pete is marrying Marcia Eldon, now can I? This way, it will look as if I threw Pete over. My announcement will be in the morning paper. And even if Marcia and Pete hurry, they can't get theirs in until the next day!"

"Is it so important?" George asked, baffled.

"Why, Pops, how you *do* talk!" Betsy's eyes were round with affected surprise. "When I've been the girl whose heart was an open book, with Pete's name on every page, and people knowing from the time I was twelve that I didn't want to marry anybody else –"

"Betsy, listen to me! You're trying to do what I warned you I wouldn't allow," Edith exclaimed in dismay.

"Oh, no, darling. I said I was going to get engaged to Bo. Now I'm telling you I'm going to marry him. And it's going to be the town's fanciest wedding. I'm going to have eight bridesmaids, and a maid of honor. I may even go so far as to have a ring bearer in a white satin suit, and a little girl to strew rose petals and stuff."

"Betsy!" wailed Edith.

"Yes, Mother?" Betsy was being very sweet, very polite, very wide-eyed.

"This is crazy. I won't let you!"

Betsy's eyes chilled. "Don't try anything, Mother, will you?" she said softly. "Because if you do, Bo and I will just drive across the state line where we can be married at the drop of a hat. I'd rather do it formally, and

117

all that – but I'm going to marry Bo, and nobody's going to stop me."

George looked from one to the other of these two women who were so dear to him, yet who seemed so much like strangers at this moment.

"But what's all the fuss?" he asked. "If you love Bo and want to marry him, I can't see any objection. Bo's a fine boy, and has a promising future, and you've known him all your life –"

"She's not in love with Bo," Edith broke in. "She hasn't the faintest intention of marrying him. She's only using him to whip Peter Marshall into line."

George muttered a mild oath under his breath, and rumpled his graying hair. "Is this true, Betsy?" he asked.

"No, Pops." Betsy smiled at him. It was a smile that was as strange and twisted as any grimace he had ever seen, and one he disliked extremely.

"Betsy, you're lying!" cried Edith. "Have you forgotten the night your father went to lodge meeting, and you unfolded your pretty little plan to me? I told you then I wouldn't let you get away with it."

"That was before I knew Peter was going to marry Marcia, so he can support her in luxury while she finishes her musical training

118

and then kicks him out," said Betsy levelly.

"Betsy! What a hateful thing to say!" protested George feebly.

"Isn't it? I'm finding out, the older I grow, that truth is seldom pretty," returned Betsy. "But that's got nothing to do with Bo and me. We're going to buy that Henderson cottage on Maple Street, and you can give us our furniture, if you like. Bo's father has already told him he'll buy us the cottage and redecorate it. And, Mother, you and I are going to be terribly busy. I want the prettiest trousseau the family exchequer – and our credit – will stand, and at least six bridesmaids and a maid of honor. Maybe I'll ask Marcia to be my maid of honor. She's very decorative, and wouldn't it be nice if she could sing? Something like 'The Voice That Breathed O'er Eden.' But of course, she isn't to be allowed to sing."

"Betsy! Will you stop chattering like a little idiot?" cried Edith. "You're out of your mind!"

A bleak look swept over Betsy's young face and her eyes seemed frightened. But the next moment the look was gone and Edith couldn't be sure she had seen it. Betsy was once more bright and airy and nonchalant.

"No, Mother, I'm *in* my mind – at last! I've been *out* of it for a long, long time.

119

You'll see. Bo and I are going to be very happy. And if you don't mind, I'd rather not talk about it any more."

She turned and ran out of the room. They heard her racing footsteps on the stairs, and a bang as her door closed behind her.

Chapter Twelve

Peter's only hope of getting Marcia alone, away from her court of admiring young friends, was to ask her to drive him out into the country. He could not see her startled look when he suggested the drive, but there was no hesitation in her voice when she answered him.

"What a grand idea, Peter," she exclaimed. "It's such a lovely afternoon and, if we drove out to the river, we might even find a breeze – who knows? Anyway, it's worth trying."

When they got up to go across the veranda and down the steps to the drive, she was surprised to see Peter put his hand on Gus' wooden harness and let Gus lead him down the steps and to the car. When Peter was settled, the dog leaped nimbly into the rumble and sat on his haunches. Gus loved to ride in a car; especially one where he could ride out in the open, as he could here.

"So you and Gus have decided to work together," said Marcia, as she slid beneath the wheel and switched on the ignition.

Peter's face tightened a little, but he answered her readily enough. "Oh, yes. I would have walked straight into a car yesterday with results that might have been tragic – though that's a debatable point – if Gus hadn't knocked me out of the way. I realized that if I'd been living up to what he expected of me, it would never have happened. So –" he shrugged – "I still feel it's a heck of a life for a fine pup, to have to drag a guy around, but I promised to make it up to him in other ways."

"I'm sure you will," said Marcia. "What a ghastly thing, Peter. You might have been killed."

"Yes," Peter agreed, without emotion. "It would be a little embarrassing to go through all the widely advertised horrors of war and then get bumped off by a car practically in your own front yard!"

"It's nothing to joke about, Peter." Marcia shuddered.

"No, I suppose not." Peter's tone said plainly that he was simply being polite, and was not at all convinced that it was not a bitter joke.

They were driving now through the outskirts of Centerville and into the open country. The day was hot, but it was late afternoon and the sun's blistering heat was faintly tempered by a hint of coming evening.

Marcia drove easily, her hands expert on the wheel. Presently, she turned the car from the paved highway into a narrow sand road that led beneath tall pines, the earth thickly dark brown with pine needles. She came out at last on a bluff above the river and parked the car. Here, the stream was wide and deep. On the banks, lusty green willows bent over, as though to admire their own grace in the mirror-like water.

"Remember this place, Peter?" asked Marcia.

"Of course. It's Pine Bluff – a favorite picnic spot for many years. I've been here thousands of times. As a cub-scout, later on as a full-fledged scout."

"And still later, as a young man courting his sweetheart, I have no doubt," Marcia teased. "I understand this is the town's favorite lovers' lane."

Peter grinned. "I'm glad we came here," he told her. "Somehow I have an idea that this is the one place in the world for me to say what I want to say to you."

Marcia tensed, and flung him a speculative glance. But she was sitting a little away from him, so he was not aware of her tensions. Gus had been released from his harness and was

123

racing through the woods, for the moment forgetful of his charge.

"Goodness, you sound – impressive," Marcia made herself say at last, with an attempt at lightness.

But Peter was sitting with his brow furrowed a little, as he tried to find exactly the words with which to clothe his thoughts.

"You see, Marcia," he said presently, "I know, of course, that you are young and beautiful and desirable. I know that you could have – well, any man you happened to want. I know it's presumption on my part that I could dare to hope you'd even consider marrying me."

Marcia's eyes were wide, and her breath was held suspended. But Peter went on:

"I know you're ambitious for a career that's inevitably expensive –"

"Also that I'm broke," she added bitterly.

"Darling, please let me finish. I've been all night and most of the day trying to screw my courage up to the point of saying this."

He turned to her swiftly, and she had a vague feeling that his sightless eyes were seeing far more than she wanted them to see.

"Marcia, I'm in love with you," he went on, "deeply and truly. But I know you don't love me, that – well, that you can't! The odds are stacked too heavily against that; but I thought that if you'd let me, I could make things a lot easier for you. I could take care of you, at least so far as money is concerned. And I wouldn't ask an awful lot of you; just that you'd let me be around and maybe not *mind* it too much –"

There was an almost unbearable humility in his voice, and Marcia said, "Stop belittling yourself, Peter! I'm very fond of you!"

He leaned toward her, his face radiant. Impulsively, she put out her hands, framed his face between them, and set her mouth on his.

His arms gathered her close and held her so tightly that for a moment she had to fight down the desire to free herself. She had been touched with pity – she had acted impulsively – but the strength of his arms that held her so tightly aroused in her a sudden surge of resentment.

She disliked being touched, caressed; she was by no means demonstrative; in fact, she was essentially cold, her whole heart wrapped up in her career and her ambitions. But she held herself still, and Peter sensed nothing of her instinct for withdrawal.

"Oh, darling, darling," he said at last. "I can't believe it. It's too wonderful. I'd hoped that I could – well, sell you a bill of goods, make a sort of bargain with you; that you'd let me look after you, and that maybe some day you might grow a little fond of me. I never dared to dream that you loved me."

Marcia hesitated a moment before she asked, "You were going to put it on a sort of business basis? You thought I would accept such a proposition?"

"I didn't dare hope you'd be interested in anything else," he acknowledged. "I think I fell in love with your voice the first time I heard it, and I've been falling deeper and deeper ever since. But I didn't have the colossal conceit to think you'd ever care anything about me. I hoped I could offer you material advantages that would offset having a husband who is – blind."

"You're very sweet, Peter," murmured Marcia.

"So are you!"

"But, Peter, I've got to be honest with you," she told him, reluctantly. "I'm terribly self-centered. I don't think I could ever love any man enough to be willing to give up my hope of a career."

"Why should you? Darling, I want to help you realize that ambition."

"You'd never be jealous? Music is a very demanding profession, Peter, if one wants to be really great – and I'm going to be." She said this with a quiet self-confidence that

126

might have startled a man less deeply in love.

"Jealous? Of your career? When I want to do everything in the world that I can to further it?"

"There's another thing, too," she said after a moment. "I've been married, Peter. You know that. Everybody in Centerville knows it. What they don't know is that my husband let me divorce him because he got tired of my using all the money I could lay my hands on for lessons, and letting the household bills go until we were being sued right and left. I want you to know the whole truth, Peter."

He laughed. "If you're trying to frighten me, sweet, you're wasting your time," he told her, undisturbed by her confession. "Every cent I have in the world is yours – with my blessing. It's nothing compared to what you are giving me. Marcia – I love you so much!"

It was dusk when they left the little pine glade above the river. Marcia left Peter in front of the Marshall place, and drove away into the deepening twilight, as he and Gus went up the drive.

Mrs. Marshall, fighting down her anxiety because Peter was out later than she had expected, trying to remind herself that darkness meant nothing to him and that he was merely idling somewhere, met him at the

127

door. She tried to disguise her sharp relief at sight of him, to hide it behind a gentle reminder that he was late for dinner.

"Mrs. Marshall," he told her gaily, his arms about her, "I have some news for you."

"Oh – then someone has told you? Perhaps I should have warned you."

Peter looked puzzled. "Told me what?" he demanded.

"That Betsy is engaged," she blurted it out, watching him anxiously.

"Betsy Drummond? That infant? Why, that's absurd!"

"Darling, we all keep trying to tell you that Betsy is quite grown up – she's almost nineteen – and Bo Norris is twenty-four."

Peter grinned. "Oh, well, then, I'll give 'em my blessing," he said generously, and laughed again.

"That wasn't the news you had for me?" asked his mother.

"You mean about Betsy's engagement? Nope, my news is about *my* engagement!"

Mrs. Marshall stood very still, and Peter, his arm about her, sensed the little shock that sped over her. Before she could check the words she had said, "Oh, Peter, *not* Marcia?"

Peter's arm dropped from her waist and he stood straight before her, the radiance leaving his face, his jaw setting a little.

"I'm happy beyond words, Mother, to tell you that Marcia has consented to marry me," he announced stiffly. "I may as well add that I feel that makes me one of the luckiest men alive."

"But, Peter, she's – well, she's *older!*" Mrs. Marshall put both shaking hands over her mouth. "I'm sorry, dear. That's not important, is it? After all, if you are fond of her –"

"I'm deeply in love with her, Mother. That she's willing to marry me is the finest thing that ever happened to me."

"Then – I'm terribly glad for you. And for me, too. Whatever makes you happy, darling, means happiness for me. You know that," said Mrs. Marshall.

But there was still a hint of constraint between them, though Peter grinned at her and said, "Thanks, Mom!"

He went up the stairs, one hand lightly touching the balustrade, the other guiding his cane.

Chapter Thirteen

Marcia was on the side veranda the following morning, dawdling dispiritedly after the light breakfast of coffee and fruit juice that was all she allowed herself, when Betsy came in.

"Oh, hello," said Marcia. Then, when she saw the girl's taut face and blazing eyes: "Why, what's wrong? You look upset."

"So you finally pulled it off," exclaimed Betsy. "Congratulations!"

Marcia sat back down in her wicker chair and eyed Betsy coolly.

"I suppose you mean Peter," she said.

"What else *would* I mean?"

Marcia shrugged. "I can't see why you are so upset. After all, since you are going to marry Bo Norris, why should you mind what happens to Peter?"

Betsy drew a long, deep breath and her hands were clenched tightly at her sides. "But I do mind what happens to Peter," she said. "I mind very much. That's why I've come to tell you that if you hurt him or make him unhappy, I'll probably try to kill you."

"Don't be melodramatic, Betsy. You're

130

not the type." Marcia's voice was a deliberate goad.

"Do you love Peter?" demanded Betsy.

"Would I be marrying him otherwise?"

"Of course you would – and it was a silly question to begin with, because I knew the answer long before I asked it," answered Betsy. "You're marrying Peter – exactly as I told him you would, if he asked you – because you're broke and he has money."

Marcia stiffened with anger. "You told Peter?"

Betsy nodded. "He had some crazy idea that he wasn't worthy of you. That's funny, isn't it?" There was youthful bitterness and venom in her voice. "Because of course you'd jump at the chance of marrying anybody who had money enough to guarantee that darned career of yours."

Marcia was on her feet now, her eyes blazing.

"Really, Betsy, even your youth is no excuse for this sort of impertinence. I think you had better go, don't you?"

"Oh, I'm going, but not until I've said what I've come to say. And that is, Peter is completely mad about you, and you can do anything you want with him. I'm hoping you are decent enough to give him an even break. Or is that asking too much? When you've used up his money and you've got where you want to go, don't kick him out, will you? Unless, by then, he's had enough of you and has learned what you're really like."

"You are unforgivable."

"What the heck do I care about your forgiving me? Nothing you could do to me could hurt me. But if you hurt Peter –" Betsy's voice broke off in a little sob.

"There's nothing you can do, Betsy, and I'd much rather you'd run along home now, if you don't mind. Peter has asked me to marry him."

Betsy nodded. "Of course. I knew he would, the minute he was sure he could give you the things you want. It's just that I thought maybe, if I tried to make you understand what a grand person he is, you might be a little more kind to him. But I suppose I'm just wasting time. You couldn't give a thought to anybody but yourself, ever!"

She turned and went out, blinded by tears.

Mrs. Marshall gave a tea for Marcia, and her friends rallied around, so it was a pleasant social affair. Afterwards, at Peter's and his mother's insistence, Marcia stayed on for dinner. It was while Peter was feeding Gus that the two women had a few moments alone.

Mrs. Marshall had planned for these few moments and had braced herself for them. She and Marcia were in the sun parlor, with its windows wide open to the late afternoon sunlight.

"I thought," Mrs. Marshall said presently, "that we might look over the house and select the rooms you and Peter would like as a suite. I'll have the remodeling and redecorating done while you are on your honeymoon."

Marcia, who had been concealing her restless boredom all afternoon, looked up sharply.

"You mean you expect us to live *here?*"

"Why, yes," Mrs. Marshall said hesitantly. "I didn't think you'd want to go on living in the Cunningham place. And, while the housing shortage is not particularly acute in Centerville, I don't know of any available houses."

"Peter and I are going to live in New York, where I can go on with my studies. Naturally."

"Oh. I thought perhaps you were giving up your career."

"That's not likely," returned Marcia. "Not after I've come this far."

"But won't it be very difficult for you to make up for this lost year?"

"Difficult, but not impossible," Marcia

assured her. "We are going to New York on our honeymoon. There are specialists I can see there. Perhaps I've gained enough in the months I've put in here so that I won't have to lose a whole year. I shall work day and night, twenty-four hours a day, if necessary, to catch up.

"I understand." Mrs. Marshall said it quietly, but she saw with devastating clarity all the motives behind Marcia's engagement to Peter. She had glimpsed them, of course, from the first, but she had tried to deny them. Peter was such a grand person surely Marcia could love him for himself, not for what he could do for her. Surely, oh, surely, cried her heart, her boy deserved better than this. It was shameful that his love should be used simply as a stepping-stone by an ambitious, mercenary woman.

She made herself smile at Marcia. "Of course it's only natural you should prefer to live in New York," she said as pleasantly as she could. "But I hope you'll visit me occasionally. It's going to be lonely without Peter."

"Of course we will. I shall be terribly busy, but there's no reason why Peter shouldn't run down often."

Peter came back then, and there was no further chance for conversation between the two women; not for the sort of conversation Mrs. Marshall felt was so vitally necessary, and yet from which she shrank with something approaching terror.

With two weddings coming so close together – Bo and Betsy had settled on a date two weeks later than the one chosen by Marcia and Peter – Centerville was in a dither. Despite the August heat, there were many parties; showers for both brides; luncheons, teas, dinners, dances. The two couples were thrown together almost constantly, since the parties were given by the same group, and everything was very gay.

Edith watched Betsy during this hectic period, an increasing fear in her heart. Outwardly Betsy was gay, breathlessly happy, chattering like mad, racing through the house like a strong wind; dashing in to change clothes, or hurrying out for some appointment. But she kept her mother at arm's length with a skill that would have done credit to a woman many years older.

Bo went around in a happy daze. Edith, watching him, felt impelled to offer advice – and acted on it before her more sober thought could check her.

On the evening when Betsy was dressing for the dinner dance that Mr. and Mrs.

Norris were giving for their prospective daughter-in-law, Bo arrived early. He was wearing his new tuxedo, his immaculate linen, and his hair was wetly plastered down. In an hour, or less, his hair would dry and spring into the hated curls that defied anything but the sternest of wet brushes, which only added to Bo's disarmingly boyish manner.

"Bo," said Edith impulsively, "there's something I feel you ought to know."

Bo's radiance dimmed a little. "You mean that I'm sort of – well, second-choice with Betsy, Aunt Edith?" he asked, like the little boy who had called her that since childhood.

"You know –?"

Bo's smile was wry now. There was nothing radiant about it. "About Pete Marshall? Sure. I've known all along. But Betsy is willing to marry me, and I'm going to do everything in my power to make her happy. If Pete is married and out of town, maybe I'll get my innings later on."

There were tears in her eyes, but Edith smiled at him. "You're a dear, Bo. But I can't feel it's quite fair to you. I mean – well, after all –" She stopped, realizing that she had almost added, "You deserve something better than being caught on the rebound."

Bo had guessed what she meant, and his

grin deepened a little. "Look, Aunt Edith," he said, "I've been in love with Betsy since we were kids. The time she let me carry her books home from school was a big moment for me. It didn't matter a bit that I knew Peter had chased her home from tagging after him, and that she was just using me to try to make him sore. You see, I didn't have a lot of pride where Betsy was concerned. And I haven't been able to acquire much, since then."

He was silent for a moment; then he added, "Don't worry about me, Aunt Edith, and don't worry about Betsy. I'll take care of her and do my level best to make her happy."

Edith sniffed, because she didn't want to break down and weep in front of him. "You young idiot," she exclaimed. "I'm not in the least worried about your making her happy. I just hope she will make you happy."

Betsy was in the doorway, a slim young flower in a frock of pale blue tulle that billowed about her high-heeled silver sandals. There was an odd look in her eyes, but she said gaily to Bo:

"Sorry I had to keep you waiting so long, darling, but I know Mother has been entertaining you. Shall we go?"

The expression in Bo's eyes, as he sprang

to his feet, was one of complete adoration. As he went out in the hall to open the door, Betsy lingered a moment to say:

"Thanks, Mother, for being so loyal. I appreciate it."

Edith flushed beneath the sting in Betsy's words, but she answered defensively, "You're not in love with him, dear."

"Good night, Mother. Don't wait up. I may be pretty late."

And over Betsy's head, Bo smiled and said again, "Don't worry, Aunt Edith. I'll take good care of her."

"I'm sure you will," returned Edith, and the door closed behind them.

Chapter Fourteen

On the day following the engagement to Peter, Marcia had written Lucy Cunningham the news. She had not written hastily nor carelessly. She had torn up half a dozen letters before she managed one to her satisfaction. She knew Lucy so well! And after she had mailed the letter, she had waited anxiously for an answer. But as the days sped by and the date she and Peter had chosen for their wedding came closer and closer, she began to fear that she had not been as clever as she had thought.

It was a morning just four days before the wedding date when Lucy's answer came.

Marcia:

Have you lost your mind? Are you mad? You must be even to think of such a thing as to marry a blind man. What if he is comfortably off and can help you with your music? You must know that I simply will not stand for it! I have great plans for you and your voice. You must have known that when I sent you off down there to that dreadful place to rest! And I certainly don't propose to have you throw everything away.

You are to return to New York immediately – do you understand? I have arranged a fund at the bank, sufficient to pay for your training. You can pay it back later if you like, or you can use it to help someone else. Anyway, I simply won't have you spoiling your life with another foolish marriage!

I have taken a house in Taxco, for the winter. You and I will go there – Mexico is enchanting! In the spring we will return to New York, and you can go on with your studies. Wire me when you will arrive, so I can have someone meet you. I was in Maine when your letter came, and that is the reason I have not written earlier. Hurry back, darling! I've missed you. You are the only amusing person I know, and we will have fun in Taxco – or if we get bored, Mexico City is quite gay.

Fondly,

Lucy

P.S. – Don't try to tell me any nonsense about being in love with this blind man. I know it isn't true! You couldn't possibly be!

Marcia dropped the letter in her lap and sat very still for a while, trying to control the

140

shaking of her hands. Lucy had come through handsomely! Marcia knew that if she had gone to Lucy frankly and asked for a loan large enough to take care of her training, she would have refused it. Lucy liked the feeling of being very generous – and she could be at times. But it had to be at her own impulse. She could never be coerced, or even cajoled. She alternated fits of generosity with fits of extreme parsimony. There were times when she was fond of the world, and generous to a degree, but there were other times when she announced bitterly that she hadn't a real friend, and that people hung about her only because they had designs on her money. And at such times, her big luxurious apartment, or any one of the many country places she maintained, was not a pleasant place.

Marcia looked down at the letter and drew in a deep breath. Lucy had at last done the thing she had hoped for, and had not dared ask. Lucy had established a fund for her musical training! And now she, Marcia, was free.

She would have to tell Peter the truth, of course, and that wasn't going to be easy. But there was a hard little core of honesty in her, surprising, perhaps, to those who knew her best. She would not lie to Peter nor pretend.

She had a liking for neat finishes; there must be no loose ends dangling. Peter loved her – she was honestly sorry that she must hurt him. But the kindest thing, in the long run, would be the brutal thing now. She would tell him straight out, frankly and flatly, that she no longer needed him and that she would not even consider marrying him.

Marcia was in her room, packing, when she heard the tap of Peter's cane on the veranda. She went down the stairs as he stepped into the hall, and he turned swiftly toward her. She saw his face light up with a smile, as he released Gus and let him go outdoors.

"Hello, darling!" he said, moving to take her into his arms.

Marcia evaded him easily. "Let's go into the living room, Peter," she suggested.

"Fine with me," Peter spoke lightly, but there was a hint of anxiety in his face, because her tones had been slightly strained.

"What I have to say is not going to be pleasant, but I hope you won't mind too much," said Marcia. Before he could answer, she added, "I've changed my mind, Peter. I can't marry you."

He stood very still, a foot or two away from her, and she saw his face grow taut.

"Of course not, Marcia," he said

142

presently. "I think I knew that from the first. But I was fool enough to let myself hope. It's because I'm blind, of course."

"No, Peter, it's not that." Marcia tried to sound convincing. "It's that – well, I had a letter from Lucy Cunningham this morning. She wants me to spend the winter with her in Mexico. She has established a fund that will guarantee my musical training –"

"And you don't need me any more," Peter finished.

"If that's the way you want to put it."

"There's no other way to put it."

"I'm sorry, of course," she said stiffly.

"You needn't be. It's only what I should have expected."

"Well, after all, you said yourself, when you asked me to marry you, that you didn't expect me to be in love with you," she reminded him.

"But you insisted you were."

"I tried."

"Thanks. I don't appreciate that very much, somehow," he cut in. "I'm delighted to know that you are going to be taken care of, and I'm sure you'll be very happy."

He turned, and felt with the tip of his cane for the way to the door. Outside, in the hot morning sunlight, he whistled for Gus, who came leaping to his side. Peter snapped the

143

wooden harness into place and he and Gus set out.

Professor Hartley turned his head, listening intently, as he caught the sound of an approaching footstep. A moment later, he said eagerly:

"Peter – good morning! This is a pleasant surprise!"

"Thanks, sir."

Peter dropped into a chair, released Gus, and lit a cigarette.

"Something's wrong, Peter," said Professor Hartley.

Peter's mouth tightened a little and he hesitated. Then:

"I'm not sure about it, Professor. Maybe something's been wrong, but now it's right. I've been walking and doing a lot of thinking. I seem to be able to think straight this morning for the first time in a long time. Marcia," he added, "has broken our engagement."

"I – I scarcely know what to say, Peter."

"Why not say what everybody else in town will be saying – that it's no more than should have been expected; that I was a fool to think a girl like Marcia Eldon would tie herself down to a blind man."

"You know that's not what people will say.

144

It's a bitter blow to you, and I'm terribly sorry, but you can face up to it, Peter. It's another challenge."

"Sure, I know," said Peter. "It's funny, but somehow it's not as devastating as I'd thought it would be. It's a blow, of course, but I think I must have been expecting it. I don't think I ever really believed she'd go through with it. It seemed too much luck for a man in my position."

The professor was silent, realizing that it was a relief to Peter to talk; to empty from his mind all the thoughts that had gathered there during the last few weeks, sure that Professor Hartley, sharing with him the blight of blindness, would understand.

"I think, too, I dreaded the thought of leaving Centerville, and living in a New York apartment," Peter went on. "Even if you can't see, there are many compensations for a blind man in a little town like Centerville that would be missing in New York. And I knew Marcia wouldn't have much time for me there, because she would be busy with her studies. Somehow, I'm a little annoyed at myself to find that I don't feel as badly as I might have."

"I'm sincerely glad for that, Peter."

"Thanks, sir. I was sure you'd understand," said Peter, and they sat for a long time in companionable silence. . . .

In the Drummond living room, Edith was saying to Betsy, "I hear Marcia's leaving town – alone."

"Who said she was leaving?" Betsy asked.

"*She* told me. She came to say goodbye," Edith said.

Edith felt her mistake even as she spoke.

Chapter Fifteen

Betsy flung open the screen door of the Cunningham place and looked about her. "Marcia?" she said.

"I'm upstairs, Betsy," Marcia's voice called. "Come on up."

Betsy ran up the stairs. Marcia stood at the door of her bedroom, slim and tall in a dark red housecoat, her hair a little dishevelled.

"Come on in, Betsy," she said. "I'm packing."

Betsy stood in the open doorway of the big, square room, and looked about her at the obvious signs of departure. Marcia went on tucking things into her suitcase. Betsy's heart raced with a consuming anger.

"So you're walking out on him," she said.

"I can't see that it's any concern of yours," returned Marcia.

"Anything that concerns Peter concerns me, and you know it! I should have known this was what you'd do. Anything as low and crawling as you are should *look* like a worm!"

Marcia's eyes flashed. "See here, Betsy, I'm prepared to put up with a lot from you, under the circumstances, knowing your childish fondness for Peter. But this is a matter strictly between Peter and me. We've talked things over and he agrees with me."

"Of course. He would agree with anything you suggest, because he's mad about you, and you're completely unscrupulous. I feel responsible for this, because I persuaded Pete to propose to you!"

"You persuaded him?" Marcia laughed. "That's quite interesting, Betsy. Peter wanted to propose to me. Nobody had to persuade him."

"He didn't have any more sense than to fall in love with you! I told him you'd marry him like a shot because you were tired of being broke and he had money." Betsy was being deliberately insulting.

Marcia stopped packing and stood up. "Look here, Betsy, I've managed my affairs for a long time without any interference from you, and I'd prefer to go on doing it."

"I know you would. But you're not going to get away with doing this to Pete – making a fool of him. You're not only cruel. You're common – and cheap!" Betsy's voice wavered on the last word, because the tears were so close. It was not in her code to cry in the face of an enemy.

"I think you've said enough," Marcia said

hotly. "Peter and I have talked things over, and we've agreed that this is the best way to adjust things. It doesn't concern you in the least."

"Anything that concerns Pete, concerns me."

"Oh, stop making a fool of yourself," snapped Marcia. "Haven't you any pride? You've made yourself a laughingstock in town, by running after Peter. You've thrown yourself at him until the poor man is half crazy trying to dodge you. I wouldn't be a bit surprised if he became engaged to me just in the forlorn hope that it might get you out of his hair! Peter isn't in love with you. He's certainly made it plain enough. Why don't you let him alone? I think he was relieved at being released from his engagement, now that you're going to marry Bo—"

Betsy stared at her in helpless fury, and suddenly Marcia began to laugh. It was then that Betsy's hand found the heavy cut-glass vase on the table beside her. Before she realized what she was doing, she had thrown it, with all her strength, straight at Marcia's face.

Marcia saw the heavy missile coming and moved swiftly to dodge it, but her foot slipped on the highly polished floor. The little bedside rug skidded, and she fell forward, striking her temple on the bed post.

The crash of the vase, and the sound of Marcia's body falling came almost simultaneously. Marcia lay quite still, face down, and Betsy stood, for a stunned moment, staring down at her.

Betsy drew a shaking hand over her eyes, and quickly phoned a doctor. Then she turned and crept down the stairs and out of the house.

Some instinct sent her to Professor Hartley. There was no thought in her mind of going home. She must get to the professor and pour out her troubles to him.

She reached the professor's place with the feeling of having come to a sanctuary. She ran along the drive and to the garden where she knew her old friend would be at this time of the day.

Peter and Professor Hartley, sitting in companionable silence, turned at the sound of her footsteps. The professor was on his feet before she reached him.

"Betsy," he cried. "Betsy, what's wrong?"

"Oh, Pete!" She swayed a little and clung to the back of the chair from which Pete had risen. "Oh, Pete – Professor – I've killed her. And I'm not sorry! I'm glad –"

"*Betsy!*" exclaimed Peter. "What are you

trying to say to us?" He put an arm around her and began patting her shoulder. "Betsy, get hold of yourself. Pull yourself together. What do you mean – you've killed her?"

"Betsy, sit down," said the professor after a moment, and poured a glass of water from the thermos bottle on the table. "Drink this, child."

Betsy's shaking hands grasped the glass, but it rattled against her teeth as she tried to drink. She looked up at the anxious, sightless faces above her and made a terrific effort to get herself under control.

"I know I shouldn't. I suppose I should be terribly sorry," she stammered at last. "But I'm not. It was high time somebody did it. She wasn't fit to live – because of what she did to you, Pete!"

Peter knelt beside her chair and took her trembling hands in his. "Listen, kid," he said, "you're talking crazy. Now draw a deep breath, count ten, and start all over again. You never killed anybody – or anything – in your life."

"Yes, I did, Pete. Maybe I didn't really mean to. But she was saying such awful things, and there was a heavy glass bowl of flowers on the table. It weighed a ton, just about – and before I knew what I was doing, I threw it at her!"

151

"Good Lord!" said Peter, under his breath.

"The bowl didn't hit her," Betsy went on miserably. "She sort of ducked. She was standing on one of those little rugs beside the bed, packing her suitcase. The floors are always waxed like glass. She ducked, and her foot slipped. She fell against the foot of the bed."

She hid her face against Peter's shoulder. Professor Hartley stood up, with a little murmur, and moved toward the house.

"Here, here, Betsy," Peter said gently, "stop drowning me! You're crying all over my nice clean shirt – and you know how easily white shirts get dirty. Snap out of it, youngster. This whole thing is a mistake. You're imagining things."

"No, Pete." She sat up and mopped her eyes with a sodden scrap of a handkerchief. "Marcia told Mom she was leaving for New York. I went over to see. Marcia was getting packed, and – well, I guess I said some pretty hateful things. But they were the truth, Pete. She's lower than anything that crawls, for walking out on you."

"Betsy," said Peter a trifle wryly, "if only I could convince you that I am old enough to manage my own affairs –"

"You never seem to realize that I'm old enough to manage mine."

Peter grinned. "Well, this fantastic tale you are telling me, my pet, certainly doesn't make you seem very grown up, if I may say so."

"You may say anything to me you like, any time, anywhere, and I'll love it," said Betsy. "Because I love you."

"Betsy, you're forgetting something."

"I don't think so."

"You were just giving Marcia a nice going-over for breaking her engagement to me because it suited her convenience. Aren't you forgetting that you are engaged to Bo?" Peter pointed out.

"Oh, but that's *different.*"

"Why is it? Just because I'm blind?"

There was a moment of silence, and then Peter said, "Don't you see, Betsy! I don't want any special favors just because I'm blind. If Marcia wanted to break her engagement to me, I am grateful that she did it exactly as she would have done it if I'd had two good eyes. Nothing could be more gruelling to any man than to know that a woman married him out of pity. If a woman really loves a man, the fact that he is handicapped isn't too important. But to marry him just because she is sorry for him

153

– Betsy that's the unforgivable thing. Marcia was completely honest with me, and I'm grateful to her."

"But if you were in love with her –"

"That's just the point," said Peter quietly. "If I had been in love with Marcia, my heart would be – well, maybe not broken, but at least permanently damaged. I acknowledged a little while ago that my first feeling was one of relief. I think I was just grateful to her because she treated me exactly as she treated the other fellows. I guess I let myself be fooled into thinking it was love. The first time I kissed her and held her in my arms, there was a queer, let-down feeling. And I dreaded the thought of leaving Centerville, of living in a New York apartment, among strangers, who would inevitably be Marcia's friends, not mine. Finally I had the uneasy suspicion that I had deluded myself, but I couldn't see any way out. Now do you begin to see why I wasn't upset when Marcia broke the engagement?"

"And I *killed* her, because I thought she'd hurt you terribly! And I was glad."

"Betsy, you lawless little idiot!" said Peter helplessly.

Professor Hartley was coming back from the house, moving surely, swiftly, his face alight.

154

"It's all right, Betsy. She's not seriously injured," he said. "She has a bad bruise on her temple, and she was knocked out for a few minutes. But the doctor has just left, and he said she would be able to travel by tomorrow, at the latest."

"Thank heaven!" said Peter.

Betsy stared at Professor Hartley, afraid to believe. "But –" she stammered.

"I talked to your mother," said the professor. "I called Marcia's and your mother came to the telephone. I told her you were here and that you were worried about Mrs. Eldon. She sounded quite upset, but she told me that the doctor is sure Mrs. Eldon is going to be all right."

Betsy drew a deep, hard breath. "I guess I was mistaken. I didn't think I minded injuring her – even killing her. But now – oh, I'm so ashamed of myself!"

"I should think you would be," announced Peter. "Betsy, I had no idea you were so explosive."

"Neither did I," admitted Betsy humbly. "I didn't intend to throw things. I just, well, she was grinning and making fun of me, saying I was making a fool of myself – and of you. Then, suddenly the vase was sailing through the air."

Peter made no comment, and presently
155

Professor Hartley said, "I think we'd all relish something cold to drink. Sit still, Betsy. I can get it."

After he had gone back to the house, Betsy and Peter sat for a moment in a silence that neither seemed to know how to break. At last Betsy spoke, saying in her usual forthright fashion, "Peter, *have* I embarrassed you by letting people know I love you?"

"Don't be a little chump, Betsy. How could any man be embarrassed by such a thing? Any man would be proud to know you thought you cared for him," said Peter.

"Will you please stop saying 'thought'! I don't *think* anything about it. I *know!*"

"And what about Bo?" Peter asked.

Color burned in her face but she still looked straight at him. "I'm sorry about Bo. Only I wasn't ever in love with him."

"Yet you wanted to hurt Marcia for being engaged to me without being in love with me."

She hesitated. Then: "I know. I called Marcia a worm. I'm even lower," she admitted. "I lost my head, I guess, when you told me you were in love with Marcia. I rushed off in all directions – and there was Bo. He thought I was pretty wonderful. I guess that soothed my hurt pride. But maybe

156

I really haven't got much pride, or I'd stop hounding you, wouldn't I?"

"You're not hounding me, Betsy. It's only that – well, during the years when you and I would normally have been falling in love with each other, I was halfway around the world, and you were here. Your love for me grew out of your memories of me. Since I've been home, you've been all steamed up over my being blind, and your burning desire to make it up to me. You see, Betsy, how well I understand you."

And Betsy, listening to him, knew that she could do nothing, knew that she could not make him change his mind. He would never understand that her love did not spring from pity, or mere hero worship. There was nothing she could do about it.

"I'd better go. Tell Professor Hartley I'll see him again soon."

Brushing Peter's restraining hand aside, she went running across the lawn and down the drive. She was walking slowly along the street toward home when a car slid to the curb, and she looked up to see Edith behind the wheel. Edith was obviously angry, but her voice was quite steady as she said, "Get in, Betsy."

"You needn't have come for me, Mother."

"I was a little afraid of what you might do

if you were left to get home alone," said Edith, and sent the car rushing up the street.

She did not speak again until they were in Betsy's room upstairs, and then she said, "Betsy, I can't tell you how shocked I am, or how disappointed I am in you. You've done a terrible thing, a disgraceful thing. Do you realize that you might easily have killed Marcia?"

Betsy shivered, but she answered with her usual devastating honesty, "I think maybe I wanted to kill her."

"Betsy!" Edith gasped. "Oh, what am I going to do with you?"

Betsy tried to grin, but it wasn't a success. "I guess maybe you'd better give me back to the stork that brought me." She struggled hard for a flippancy far removed from her real feelings.

Chapter Sixteen

George had finished breakfast and gone. Edith, lingering at the table over her second cup of coffee, tensed a little as she heard Betsy's footsteps in the hall. But she looked up, smiling, as the girl came in. Betsy was looking very young and very lovely in blue linen shorts and halter, the beloved saddle shoes and socks on her sunburned feet.

She greeted Edith with what tried hard to be a gay grin.

Edith pretended to be absorbed in the morning paper, after she had brought Betsy's breakfast. Then she stole a glance at her daughter's face and asked lightly, "Well, what is it now?"

Betsy frowned. "Mother, could I go away for a while?" she asked.

"Running away, dear?"

"I guess so," answered Betsy honestly. "I – well, I told Bo I couldn't marry him. He was sweet about it, and I felt like a worm."

"So now you'd like to run out and let him bear the unpleasantness alone."

Betsy flung up her head and, though the

159

color flamed in her cheeks, she cried out defensively, "Mother, you and Dad have been perfectly swell, but aren't you two just a little bit to blame? I never had much of a chance to grow up. You never let me make any decisions – important ones. You were anxious to protect me, and I love you for it, and I'm grateful. Only – well, I thought maybe you'd let me go to Atlanta and get a job and make my own living for a while and learn to stand on my own feet. After all, how else can I ever be grown up?"

Edith was appalled, yet she was honest enough to admit there was truth in what Betsy said. She and George had, to the best of their ability, wrapped the child in protecting layers of cotton wool; they had shielded her, perhaps too much.

"But, darling, you haven't any business training," she pointed out.

"I can be a salesgirl in a department store, or a five-and-ten. They train girls for that. And I'd be earning my own living and sort of coming to grips with real life." Betsy's voice was so eager, her sincerity so obvious, that the absurd little phrase did not sound at all funny. "I'd stay with Aunt Sally. She could tuck me away somewhere in a corner. I'll sleep on a shelf in the linen closet, if necessary. I'll pay her board, and live on what was left. I don't want any allowance from home. I want to support myself and find out what it's really like to be on my own. Mother, *please!*"

In the end, when even George had to give in to her pleading and planning, Betsy departed for Atlanta. While Centerville gossiped, and some people condemned her for the treatment of Bo, others defended her because, they argued, everybody had known all along that Peter Marshall was the man Betsy loved. Bo should have expected nothing better.

Edith, her mouth a thin line, her eyes harassed, returned wedding presents and apologized to friends who had given parties for Betsy – and wished heartily that she, too, could slip out of Centerville and hide somewhere until people had forgotten.

The pretty little house that Bo had prepared for his bride was sold at an excellent profit to a home-hungry family; Anne Gray took up where she had left off with Bo, when Betsy came along, and people nodded and decided that Bo was consoling himself very nicely.

Peter spent many hours with Professor Hartley and, as their friendship grew, it came to mean a great deal to both men. Gradually, Peter became more reconciled to his physical handicap – and more independent, as his and Gus' understanding deepened.

September passed, with Edith watching eagerly for Betsy's letters. Betsy had found work in one of the big department stores. She wrote excitedly about her days "in training school" until at last she was allowed "on the floor, to sell." She loved the city with its crowds and its noise and its color. She had made friends in the store, as well as among Aunt Sally's boarders, and she was happier than she had dreamed she could be.

Edith tried hard to read between the lines things that might be there: little signs of homesickness; traces of loneliness; of regret. But Betsy's letters were unfailingly gay, and the brief notes Edith received from Aunt Sally reassured her of her daughter's well-being. Besides, Betsy would surely come home for Thanksgiving – and it was October, now.

The calendar said there were only thirty-one days in October. Frankly, Edith doubted it. She was quite sure that it was twice as long as any month had a right to be. The house seemed terribly big, and it echoed with a silence, ached with emptiness. Where once she had sighed a little with irritation at the incessant sound of footsteps and laughter and youthful voices, where she had sometimes

162

wished that a radio had never been invented, she sat now in a silence that was almost unbearable.

"What wouldn't I give," she told herself, "to have Betsy and her crowd back, running through the house, raiding the icebox, kicking back the rugs to dance, the telephone ringing like mad. . . ."

At such times, when the loneliness seemed almost more than she could bear, she would get out Betsy's letters and read them again. Then she would tell herself that it was best for Betsy to be away just now, even though it was terribly lonely for her parents.

It was a great disappointment to Edith when Betsy wrote that she could not come home for Thanksgiving. The store would be closed for only one day, Betsy explained; she would spend more of her time on the road than she would be able to spend at home. But she had been promised an extra two days at Christmas, she would come home then. With that, Edith and George had to be content. . . .

Christmas came at last, just when Edith was convinced it never would. Since Christmas fell on Tuesday, Betsy had managed to get the Monday before as well as the Wednesday after. And so she left Atlanta Sunday morning and was in Centerville shortly after noon.

George and Edith had been pacing the platform for half an hour before the first plume of smoke, announcing the train's approach, was visible down the line. When the train slid to a halt, and a girl in a smart blue suit, a topcoat swung jauntily about her shoulders, her hair in a very sophisticated upswept arrangement, appeared at the top of the steps, Edith burst into tears.

"Hello, you two! Is this any way to greet the return of the prodigal daughter?" protested Betsy. But she wept a little herself as she clasped her mother close and reached out a hand to her father.

"Oh, Betsy, I'm so glad to see you," said Edith, smiling through her tears.

"Maybe you think I'm not happy to see you!" Betsy grinned at both of them. "I never realized before what a handsome pair of parents I have!"

They got into the car and drove home, with Betsy chattering like mad; regaling them with gay little tales of her adventures, of her friends, of her work. The house was bright with holly and mistletoe and the lovely greens that are at their best in this mild winter climate. There was also the rich, spicy odor of Edith's good cooking.

Edith and George smiled at each other as Betsy's flying feet raced up the stairs. The telephone, as though it had just been waiting for her arrival, burst into clamorous demands for attention. And by dinner time on Sunday night, it was almost as though Betsy hadn't been gone at all. The house was echoing with laughter and young voices; the radio was going full blast, and somebody was yelling that there was a new Sinatra record – and why didn't they turn the television off so they could play it on the phonograph.

Once George and Edith might have retired before the clamor, but tonight they loved it. George displayed an unexpected ability to jitterbug, and the whole evening was as merry as a traditional Christmas season should be.

They were laughing so hard that nobody heard the doorbell ring. Then the door was opened, letting in a breath of cold air, and a man stood on the threshold – directly beneath a huge spray of mistletoe whose pearl-like berries shimmered in the yellow light.

"Sounds like a swell party," he called. There was a moment of confusion, followed by a brief silence. Then:

"Pete!" cried Betsy. She ran to him, flung herself in his arms and kissed him joyously.

"Welcome home," said Peter, and laughed.

Betsy's face flamed. "Oh, well, if you just *will* stand beneath the mistletoe, you should know what to expect," she told him. "Up and at him, girls!"

The girls clustered about Peter and the boys complained loudly that they hadn't been smart enough to take advantage of the mistletoe.

"Is that starting all over again?" George whispered to Edith.

"What ever gave you the impression it had stopped?" murmured Edith.

It was an hour or more before Edith, moving among the guests, assuring herself of their comfort and well-being, discovered that Peter and Betsy were missing. And when she did, she only drew a deep breath and sighed. . . .

Chapter Seventeen

Christmas, in Centerville, is a time of gray skies and "gentle-to-moderate rains," according to the local weather bureau. Snow is something so rare that when it does appear briefly, the young people are hysterical with excitement; freezes are almost equally as rare. The usual winter-time weather is mild, with occasional bracy, chilly winds.

Tonight, as though in deference to Betsy's homecoming, was such a night. The moon was old and worn wafer-thin, and its light was pallid, like a thin wash of very old gold. The air was crisp and cold, and Betsy and Peter stood at the end of the walk, leaning on the gate.

Betsy gave a sigh of utter happiness and said, "Maybe Centerville isn't the most beautiful place in the world. Maybe it isn't big and important, but you'd have trouble convincing me it isn't!"

Peter turned his sightless eyes upon her and grinned. "Were you homesick?"

"Let's not talk about gruesome things."

They stood for a while in companionable

silence, and then Peter said, "I've missed you like the dickens, Betsy."

"Did you, Pete? I missed you, too."

Once more there was a brief silence, and Peter's voice was a little husky when he said:

"Betsy, you're sweet – and so beautiful."

Betsy stared up at him, caught by astonishment. "Pete!" she gasped. "This is *Betsy* – remember? The long-legged brat with braces on her teeth and carrots in her hair!"

Peter shook his head. "No, that was the Betsy who went to war with me! The kid who was with me every time I had a chance to think. She was the kid I talked to so I wouldn't go to sleep from sheer exhaustion on night patrols. I used to keep myself awake, when I was so tired that just sitting still was like being drugged."

"But, Pete, I never realized –"

"She used to come and talk to me," he went on, ignoring the interruption. "And well, *that* was the Betsy who was the long-legged, carrot-topped brat. I brought her back home with me. But after I got here, I found there was another Betsy. A new and disturbing Betsy."

"Disturbing?" she repeated, anxiously.

"Disturbing!" Peter returned it firmly. "A girl whose hair is like old mahogany that has been polished until it's like satin; with a skin that's delectable; a Betsy who is beautiful."

"Peter, who – I mean –"

"Bo Norris told me," he answered. "Quite a lad, Bo is. He came to see me a few days after you'd gone to Atlanta. It seems that there was something resting heavily on Bo's mind. He felt that – well, that complications might easily develop, and that it was his duty to clear them up before they could."

"Complications?" Betsy repeated.

Peter turned as though to look down at her, and the pale moonlight was reflected for an instant from his dark glasses.

"It seems that Bo was under no delusions about your being in love with him, Betsy. He knew very well that he was catching you on the rebound. When you said 'yes' to him the day before Marcia announced her engagement to me, Bo knew then – so he says – that you were not in love with him."

Betsy stood very still, her hands clenched about the pickets of the gate before her, her face turned away, as though he could see its expression and read there something she was not yet ready to reveal.

After a moment Peter said, "But, of course, Bo could be mistaken. Some very smart people have been."

"He wasn't mistaken," exclaimed Betsy.

"But why was it necessary for him to tell you? I'm practically worn out from throwing myself at you. I've told you about a million times how much I loved you – only you wouldn't listen!"

Peter's arms opened and she was in them. He held her close for a long moment. Then, before he kissed her, he put her a little away from him and looked down at her, as though his heart saw clearly what his eyes could not see.

"Betsy, I haven't any right to ask you to chain yourself to a man handicapped as I am." Peter's voice was grave now, almost solemn. "You're young and lovely and –"

"In love with you," she reminded him.

"Bless you for that," said Peter. "Only it's for always, Betsy," he added, "or not at all. I couldn't have you for a little while and then, if you found the going too tough, give you up. That I couldn't take."

"You'll never have to. Oh, Pete, can't you get it through that thick head of yours that I've been yours ever since the day I learned to spell 'differential' – and long before I ever knew what it meant? Oh, Peter, I forget that you are blind. It only makes me love you more, because you need me more, and there are more things I can do for you. I love you. I've always loved you. Can't you just accept that and stop torturing both of us with questions and answers that don't really mean anything?"

She was sobbing a little, and Peter's arms closed about her and held her very close. After an interval that might have been moments, or could have been hours, she looked up at him, radiant.

"Oh, Peter, what a lot of time we've wasted! It should have been like this when you stepped off the train," she told him. Then she grinned and added unexpectedly, "I adore Bo Norris."

"Oh. So it's like that, is it?"

"Next to you, I mean. Bo, bless him, made you see things you refused to see. And now – when are we going to be married?"

Peter laughed. "Wait a minute, you forward creature. *I'm* supposed to ask you that!"

"Then go ahead and ask me, so I can say tomorrow, or the next day at the very latest!"

Peter's answer was to hold her still closer in his arms. But it seemed quite enough to Betsy.